THE TRIALS OF QUINTILIAN

In ancient Rome, Marcus Fabius Quintilianus was a real barrister, honoured for being a teacher, rhetorician, jurist and a crime solver . . . In these three stories Quintilian, a character who is based on this early detective, chronicles some of the eminent man's cases. The opening tale, set in the last half of the first century AD, is 'Blind Justice' — where Quintilian must defend a blind man accused of brutal patricide . . .

MICHAEL KURLAND

---◆---

THE TRIALS OF QUINTILIAN

Complete and Unabridged

LINFORD
Leicester

First published in Great Britain

First Linford Edition
published 2012

British Library CIP Data

Kurland, Michael.
  The trials of Quintilian. - -
  (Linford mystery library)
  1. Detective and mystery stories, American.
  2. Large type books.
  I. Title II. Series
  813.5'4–dc23

  ISBN 978–1–4448–1256–5

Published by
F. A. Thorpe (Publishing)
Anstey, Leicestershire

Set by Words & Graphics Ltd.
Anstey, Leicestershire
Printed and bound in Great Britain by
T. J. International Ltd., Padstow, Cornwall

This book is printed on acid-free paper

1

Blind Justice

My name is C. Plautus Maximilianus Aureus. I will soon be twenty-two years old, and I have accomplished nothing with my life. When Alexander the Great was my age, he had conquered all of Persia. When Cicero was my age, he had tried and won his first cases before a Roman jury. But I — I have a stammer and a slight limp from a childhood illness that twisted my spine and left me just crippled enough to be useless in battle and unattractive to women. I am commonly known as 'Max the Scribbler,' or sometimes just 'Scribbler' for the way I write down everything said by my patron and mentor, the great teacher, jurist and orator Marcus Fabius Quintilianus. I carry about a great supply of wax tablets in a canvas sack for that purpose.

The instance I am relating occurred

but a few months ago, in the Spring of the second year of the reign of the Emperor Vespasian. It was then that, with many misgivings, Quintilian agreed to defend a youth named Rufus Plenius Abracius against the charge that he had murdered his own father. This was not a popular case to take on, as you can imagine; the grumbling in the Forum was that banishment was insufficient and death, unless it were a particularly lingering and painful death, was too lenient a punishment for such a crime. The fact that the accused lad was blind made the crime somehow even worse, as was the fact that his own stepmother was his accuser, and it was she who was bringing the case to trial.

The commission was brought to Quintilian by his friend Titus the shipowner, who had known Quintilian since they were boys together in the sunny hillsides of Spain. I assume Spain has sunny hillsides, why shouldn't it? The two of them sat together on the bench under the single fig tree growing in the courtyard of Quintilian's villa, which is on

2

the outskirts of Rome by the Via Sculpa. The kitchen girl brought out a pitcher of heated wine and three goblets, and the two old friends talked over the events of the week; Quintilian waiting patiently for Titus to bring up whatever had brought him along the dusty road in his sedan chair so early in the day. I sat on a stool by Quintilian's feet, ready with tablet and stylus in case Quintilian said anything worthy of recording.

'Rufus Plenius Abracius needs an advocate,' Titus said, after hemming and hawing through his first goblet of wine and refilling the vessel.

'The lad accused of killing his own father?'

Titus nodded. 'I'm afraid there'll be little glory in this for you,' he said, an understatement if I've ever heard one, 'but at least you'll get paid. I'll guarantee your fee.'

Quintilian scowled into his goblet. 'This is not a good time,' he said. 'I am devoting much of my energy to preparing notes for a book on the teaching of rhetoric and oratory to the young.'

'In addition,' I added from my place on a small stool at the foot of the bench, 'to actually teaching rhetoric to eleven youths and three advanced students. That takes up much of the week.'

They both turned to glower at me. 'They would come to the trial and watch and listen,' Quintilian said. 'They would learn much from seeing for themselves how it should be done.'

'Watching the master in action is worth many hours of classroom instruction,' Titus agreed firmly.

'Silly me,' I said. 'I abase myself.'

Quintilian turned to Titus. 'Tell me about it,' he said.

Rufus Plenius Abracius, as Titus told Quintilian, was the son of Marcus Vexianus Abracius, a grain merchant who had shipped many cargos from the wheat fields of Egypt in tub-hulled vessels owned by Titus. There had been no bad blood between father and son until the father had remarried. Indeed, some five years before, Rufus Plenius had saved his father's life in a fire, and had been blinded when he went back in an unsuccessful attempt

4

to rescue his mother.

According to Titus, Rufus Plenius had erected a shrine to his dead mother in a corner of his room and spent most of the day every day lying on his bed, weeping. Although such abject mourning was certainly unmanly, it was at least understandable, as the boy had been very close to his mother and blamed himself for her death.

The rift between Rufus Plenius and his father had grown since the father took Lucilla Collesta, a dark-haired Syracusan beauty a full two decades younger than himself, to be his new wife. The lad refused to attend the wedding and, although outwardly civil to his stepmother, had as little to do with her or his father as possible from that moment onward; going so far as to move to a room in a distant part of the house beyond the kitchens. Two servants' rooms were combined to provide him with his new quarters.

On the second day of Parentalia in February — the solemn festival for honoring dead parents — Rufus Plenius had walked more than a mile out of the city along the Via Appia to the family mausoleum where his mother's ashes lay. He had chosen to go by himself and had scorned the use of a sedan chair or the company of his body slave, although it was a chill and drizzly day and the road was rough and dangerous, even for the sighted. He had spent the night at the mausoleum, wrapped in his wool cloak, with his head resting on a convenient slab of marble.

When he returned, his stepmother had discovered a vial of poison in his shoulder bag. Whether he intended to take his own life, or attempt the life of either his father or stepmother cannot be known. The vial was taken away from him, and after that he seldom left his room.

Titus refilled his cup. 'As to the murder itself,' he went on, 'Marcus was stabbed right through the heart while he slept, one clean blow, and his son's bloody hand prints were discovered on the wall of the corridor — '

'That's very interesting,' Quintilian interrupted. 'Stabbed with what?' Then he raised his hand. 'Wait, don't go on. If I am to take this case I must at least gather the facts second-hand and not third-hand. We must go to the home of Marcus Vexianus Abracius and see for ourselves what there is to be seen and listen to what there is to be told.'

'Then you'll take the case?' Titus asked.

'First tell me why you're so willing to defend the lad,' Quintilian said. 'If we lose the case Rufus Plenius cannot inherit and will be penniless. Why are you willing to support him to the extent of guaranteeing my exorbitant fee?'

Titus thought about it for a minute and then shrugged. 'I like the lad,' he said. 'Black as the case against him seems, I cannot believe he killed his own father. It is not in his character, as I know it, to do so.'

'Then I will look into it,' Quintilian told him. 'Whether or not I'll appear in court for the lad depends on what I find.'

The next day we journeyed across Rome to the home of Rufus Plenius and his stepmother, Quintilian walking briskly the whole way and I scurrying along behind as best I could. Over Quirinal Hill and Viminal Hill we went without

7

pausing. Even the two slaves we brought along as bodyguards, great, hulking Celts from the Islands of the Mists, had trouble keeping up with him. There was a brief respite before we climbed Esquiline Hill, but only because a senator recognized Quintilian and bade him stop and answer a brief question regarding the proper raising of the senator's young nephews. Quintilian loved to walk in all weathers, claiming he could think better as he strode along. For my part, I had all I could do to breathe, and had little energy left for thinking at all.

When we arrived at the home of the deceased Marcus Vexianus Abracius the bier which had held his body still stood in the atrium, although Marcus himself had been cremated several days before and his ashes now rested with those of his first wife in the family mausoleum outside the gates of the city. It was during the procession to the funeral pyre that the grieving widow, while rending various garments in her agony, had declared her intention of having the son tried for murdering his father.

Quintilian began by interviewing Rufus Plenius in his windowless room beyond the kitchen, where the lad would remain, with a pair of guards at the door, until the trial. Quintilian sent a slave for a burning rush to light the two oil lamps in the room, since Rufus Plenius, naturally enough, was sitting in the dark.

The room was starkly furnished: nothing but a simple pallet, a stool, a chest for clothing, and a small altar in the corner holding a miniature portrait of a strikingly good looking woman and some items of jewelry. The boy was about nineteen, and handsome enough except for some small scars about his ears and neck. It wasn't until he turned his face full toward you that you got an eerie feeling of strange thoughts at work behind those white, sightless eyes. Or at least I did.

'You must cooperate with me and tell me the truth if I am to defend you,' Quintilian told the lad.

'It hardly matters,' Rufus Plenius answered listlessly, sitting cross-legged on his pallet by the back wall. 'Whether I live or die is of little importance.'

'Did you kill your father?'

'Of course not!' Rufus Plenius turned his sightless eyes toward Quintilian. 'I would not do such a thing. I honor — honored — my father.'

'But you loved your mother?'

'I did.' He turned his face toward the small altar in the corner. 'I do.'

'You disapproved of your father's remarriage?'

'He did not seek my approval, nor would it have been my place to give it. He was paterfamilias — head of the family. I was his son.'

'Yet parricide is not unheard of in Rome,' Quintilian mused. 'That's why there is a name for it. Under Roman law children are unable to marry or conduct business without their father's consent as long as he is alive, no matter what their age. Sons with a cruel or overbearing father, or merely anxious for their inheritance can be severely tempted to perform rash acts. It is among the most severely punished of crimes, yet it is not even uncommon.'

'I have no interest in marrying,' Rufus Plenius said, 'and I conduct no business.'

'You dislike your stepmother?'

The lad shrugged. 'I neither like nor dislike Madam.'

'What can you tell me of the night of the murder?'

'I slept through the night. I was awakened by rough hands grabbing at my body, and Madam's voice in the background yelling curses and imprecations. I do not know what happened or who was to blame.'

'Have you any conjectures?'

'None. My father was well liked. He did not involve himself with politics. Most murders, I believe, are political.'

'Most murders are for gain,' Quintilian told him. 'Did anyone stand to gain from your father's death?'

Rufus Plenius thought for a moment and then shook his head. 'I inherit,' he said. 'But father always gave me anything I asked for, so I had no need to kill him. Likewise, my stepmother gets the widow's portion, but father never denied her requests. So, if anything, she loses by his death, since I inherit most of the estate and she cannot expect me to be so generous.'

'Well thought out,' Quintilian commended. 'Then it is a mystery, isn't it? We must continue our examination. I will get back to you.'

'As you will,' the lad agreed listlessly.

We left the room and walked down the narrow corridor which bypassed the kitchen and led directly to the inner courtyard, with one door toward the end giving into the father's bedroom. The bloody prints of the young man's hand — well, of someone's hand — could be seen on the wall by the flickering light of the oil lamp. 'Who uses this corridor?' Quintilian asked the young household slave who was lighting our way.

'Nobody,' she told him. 'The young master used to use it to go sit in the courtyard and have the old Greek read to him. But now he doesn't leave his room.'

'Even before he was confined to his room by the guards, he stayed there?'

'Oh, yes. He didn't leave that room for nothing. Except every evening he went down this very corridor to ask his father how the day went and whether he needed anything. His father would always say the day went well, and no, thank you, and the young master would go back to his room. He stayed in the dark. Sometimes we'd hear him talking.'

'Talking?'

'Reciting, like. '*Tempus erat quo prima* — ''

'Oh, yes. Virgil. From *The Aeneid*.' Quintilian recited in his sonorous voice: ''It was the hour when the first sleep of suffering mortality begins, and, by the grace of heaven, steals on its sweetest errand of mercy.' Schoolboy memorization, but some of it may be comforting to him.'

'That damn poem!' came a woman's voice from behind the door to the master bedroom. The door swung open and a woman stood, one hand on her hip, the other leaning against the door, glaring at us. She was young, with long black hair and a heavily made-up face in the Greek fashion: dark-rimmed eyes and rouged cheeks, and heavy gold earrings. Too much for my taste, but beautiful nonetheless. She stared at us for a long minute, and then demanded, 'Who are you?'

13

'Marcus Fabius Quintilianus,' Quintilian told her. 'And this is my associate, Plautus Maximilianus Aureus. You must be Lucilla Abracius, widow of Marcus.'

'I must,' she agreed. Then she shuddered. 'Widow. I hate that word.'

He took her hand. 'Madam, I regret interrupting your grief, but there are a few questions I must ask you.'

'Of course,' she said.

He did not release her hand immediately, and she did not seem eager for him to. She squeezed his hand and then put her palm up so that she was, ever so slightly, clutching his thumb. It was an erotic gesture, and she was clearly a woman who was created for erotic gestures. She couldn't help it, it was her nature. Even I felt — well, no matter what I felt.

Quintilian looked at her hand, as though suddenly becoming aware that he had been holding it, and then released it. 'You have accused your stepson of murdering your husband,' he said. 'Do you have direct knowledge that he did so? Did you see him commit the murder?'

'No,' she said. 'Though I slept at my husband's side, I slept through whatever happened.' She shuddered again and backed into the room, dropping onto the bed. 'You'd think that the gods would have awakened me so that I could have put my own body between Marcus and the downthrust sword.'

'Then it was a sword that killed him?'

'Yes. A military short sword. It was still in his body.'

'Was it from the house?'

'I don't think so. I'd never seen it before.'

Quintilian entered the room after her and looked around. There were two doors, one to the corridor we had just quit and one to the courtyard. A large window, its shutters swung open, provided light and air. 'I know it will be difficult for you, but if you could tell me just what happened that day, it would help.'

She sat up, her posture changing from one of invitation to one of defiance. 'Help him, you mean,' she said. 'I know who you are and what you are doing here.'

'Of course you do,' Quintilian told her.

15

She paused for a second and then shook her head. 'But I suppose . . . if you could find a way to show that the boy *didn't* do it, you would please the shade of my dead husband. He always liked the boy, may the gods forgive him!'

'Just tell me what happened,' Quintilian insisted softly.

'Someone — and if it wasn't the boy I don't see who it could have been — came into the room while we slept and drove the sword through my husband's heart.'

'He didn't cry out or make a sound?'

'I'm a heavy sleeper, but not that heavy. I heard nothing.'

'There was no sign of a struggle?'

'None.'

'And then?'

'And then I awoke and rose and opened the shutters. And by the morning light coming in the window I saw my husband lying dead in the bed beside where I had slept. I screamed and ran into the corridor.'

'In this very bed?'

She shook her head. 'I had the bed destroyed on which the murder took place. There was too much blood.'

'So you ran into the corridor?'

'And I saw there, by the light through the open door, a bloody print of a hand on the wall. So I guess I screamed again, and kept screaming until a couple of the slaves came. Big, brawny men who work in the garden. They had been guarding the front door that night. I had them fetch a light and we followed the hand prints back down the corridor to Rufus Plenius's room. Then I called the city guard.'

'And you think your stepson committed this deed — murdered his father?' Quintilian asked.

The woman stared at him blankly. 'What else is there to think?' she replied.

'And you're determined to prosecute him for murder?'

'What else is there to do?'

'What indeed?' Quintilian took an oil lamp from the table and went back into the corridor to look at the hand prints. He had the slave girl hold her lamp on one side of each hand print while he held his on the other, and he peered closely at each one, making his way slowly back down the corridor. There were seven of them along the right hand wall, where someone might have put his hand on the wall for support as he blindly staggered back to his room. Seven very well delineated prints of the same right hand; all clear and heavy with blood and pointing inexorably toward the blind boy's room.

At one point Quintilian spotted something on the floor and bent down to examine it.

'What have you found?' I asked.

He stood up. 'Wax,' he said. 'Candle wax. Just a few drops. Mixed with a bit of blood, so they're recent, unless someone else has been bleeding in the corridor.' He turned to the girl. 'May I assume that these bloody hand prints are the only traces of blood that you've found in the corridor?'

'Oh, yes, sir,' she told him.

'At any time?'

'As far as I know, sir. Since I've been here, and that would be two years come the feast day of Flora this April.'

'Thank you, girl. You may lead us to the gate, now.'

And with that we went home. Titus came by the next day to see whether Quintilian would take the assignment. 'I will venture it,' Quintilian told him, 'but with no guarantee of success.'

'You don't believe the lad is innocent?'

'Only the gods can determine true innocence or guilt,' Quintilian told him. 'What matters to a Roman jury is the force of argument and how well presented it is. It's just as important to keep fifty-one Roman jurors awake as it is to convince them. I will endeavor to keep them awake.'

'But what do you think? Do you believe the lad is innocent?'

Quintilian patted him on the shoulder. 'What I think hardly matters. The jury decides who's innocent and who's guilty. The beautiful Lucilla has engaged Blasus Parenas as prosecutor, and Blasus has a slippery and well-oiled tongue. After he has finished greasing the jury with his well-chosen words we'll be lucky if I'm allowed to speak at all. They may all leap to their feet and acclaim the guilt of my client in a unanimous burst of enthusiasm.'

'You must have bad dreams,' Titus told him.

'When I'm trying a case I don't permit myself to dream.'

'But is the lad guilty or isn't he? Surely you have an opinion.'

'Oh. Your instincts were right. Rufus Plenius Abracius did not kill his father.'

'But the bloody hand prints?'

'Exactly. The bloody hand prints.'

And that was all Titus could get out of him. I, of course, did not try, curious as I was to know what my mentor had discerned, and what he thought of the case. He would merely tell me to observe and to learn. I observed, but I did not see what he saw. I learned, but he learned more. How was I ever going to be able to emulate the master when from moment to moment I had no idea of what the master was doing?

The trial commenced three weeks later. Blasus Parenas was as good as Quintilian predicted. A handsome man with long, brown hair, he wore his toga creased into precise pleats, with the end carefully folded over his arm. He called Lucilla, the stepmother, as his first witness. She had arrived in a litter carried by eight porters and preceded by a centurion in full dress uniform. She showed more leg than was proper and told the jurors how she missed her husband more every day, and how sweet and good he had been, and if Rufus Plenius didn't kill him, who could have.

Quintilian's cross examination was brief. 'Have you ever heard Rufus Plenius Abracius say anything against his father, or speak to his father in anger?'

'Well,' the good Lucilla said, trying to look as though her teeth were being pulled against her will, 'since you asked — I have heard him mutter imprecations under his breath. I believe he never forgave his father for marrying me.'

'Thank you,' Quintilian said, sitting down. I looked at him with some astonishment. He never before, to my knowledge, had led a witness into giving questions harmful to his client. But he looked satisfied, and I said nothing.

Blasus then called the two gardeners who had watched the front door that night, and received agreement that they didn't have to be questioned under torture. (The custom is dropping out of favor anyway. The emperor himself has said that a slave under torture will say whatever the torturers want to hear, and therefore his testimony is useless.) They affirmed that no one could have gotten through the door without their knowing it, and that no one at all, friend or stranger, came in that night. They were also the two who rushed to Lucilla's aid when she began screaming that morning. They testified to seeing the bloody hand prints and following them to Rufus Plenius's chamber.

Quintilian rose in cross-examination when the second one was done. 'The hand prints were easy to follow?'

'Yes, sir.'

'Good. Bold, strong hand prints, were they?'

'Yes sir?'

'And the boy, Rufus Plenius, what was he doing when you entered his room?'

'He were asleep, your honor.'

'So you had to wake him up to tell him what he did?'

'Yes, sir.'

'There was blood all over him, of course.'

'No, your honor. I didn't see no blood.'

'Thank you. That's all.'

Dr. Heraclates, who had been treating Rufus Plenius for the past year, was the next witness. 'The lad is suffering from melancholia,' he said, 'brought on by the death of his mother.'

'But his mother died two years ago,' Blasus pointed out. 'Surely Rufus Plenius should have gotten over that by now.'

'Normally yes, I would say,' Dr. Heraclates said, his white Greek beard bobbing as he spoke. 'But the lad and his mother were very close.'

'Ah!' Blasus adjusted his toga with his thumb and forefinger, getting the crease *just so* as he turned to face the jury. 'You mean to say,' he asked, his hands behind his back, his face bland, 'that Rufus Plenius Abracius had an unnatural' — he drawled out the word 'unnatural' — 'affection for his mother?'

'Well, very strong, yes.'

'Unnatural?'

'I wouldn't go that far.'

'You don't need to, Doctor,' Blasus said, with a wave of his arm leaving it for the jury's imagination to go at least that far.

Then Serpo, Rufus Plenius's own body slave, was called. Quintilian, who had been dozing, or pretending to doze, suddenly jumped to his feet. 'Come now!' he thundered. 'A slave cannot be called to testify against his own master. Surely my learned opponent knows that. The chairman of the court knows that. Everybody in this room' — and he waved his hand to take in the entire fifty-one jurors and the hundred or so onlookers — 'knows that!'

Blasus Parenas turned to Senator Claudius Aquillus, the Chairman of the Court, an elderly man with a hawk nose, piercing blue eyes, and a brain like a lawbook of Roman custom and precedent, for a ruling. 'Your honor?'

'He's right, Citizen Parenas,' Chairman Claudius said. 'Why should this slave be exempt from the established custom?'

'Technically, your honor, the slave was not Rufus Plenius's property at the time in question; Rufus Plenius's father was still alive, and so everything of which Rufus Plenius was possessed, including his slave, was, in law, his father's property. He should not be allowed a legal defense for the crime of murdering his father that is only made possible because he murdered his father.'

'Ah, but that's what you must prove!' Quintilian said. 'Can you seek to prove that my client murdered his father by bringing in evidence that is only admissible provided that he did murder his father?'

'Interesting,' Claudius said, looking from one advocate to the other. He leaned back and pondered, closing his eyes.

After a minute he opened them to look at Blasus Parenas. 'I believe that this time you've won your point, counselor, by a hair. Go on with questioning the slave.'

Quintilian leaned back on the bench and smiled benignly. 'There's nothing old Claudius loves so much as a point of law,' he murmured to me. 'I thought Blasus would have to work a little harder to get that in. Still it might throw him off his stride.'

'Is this slave's testimony damaging to our client?' I asked him in an undertone.

'I don't see how,' Quintilian murmured. 'But Blasus doesn't know that. Even now he's wondering what question I fear his asking the little slave.'

And so it proved. Serpo said all he could say that was of interest in the first three sentences: He'd been body slave to Rufus Plenius since the lad was twelve. It was he who had warned the stepmother about the poison, since he'd followed Rufus Plenius to the Mausoleum that day and watched him clutch the small vial to his chest and occasionally raise it to his lips, and then shake his head and put it away. He had on occasion heard Rufus Plenius muttering curses that might have been directed toward his father.

Quintilian stood up and interrupted. 'Those curses, you didn't hear them clearly?'

'No, sir.'

'Could have been against his father?'

26

'Yes, sir.'

'Could have been against the gods who blinded him and killed his mother?'

'Yes, I guess so, sir.'

'Could have been against himself, for being so accursed as to fail to rescue his mother?'

'Well, yes, I guess so.'

'Could have been against the green team for losing in the chariot races that day?'

'Well — ' Serpo shifted uncomfortably as the jurors chuckled.

Quintilian sat back down, and Blasus artfully ignored him and went on. He gnawed at every possible relationship that Serpo might have been privy to, convinced that there was meat in there somewhere. He came up without even a radish.

Quintilian stood again and asked, 'That sword we've heard about; did you ever see young Rufus Plenius Abracius with a sword?'

'No, sir.'

'Did his father have any swords that you know about?'

'No, sir.'

27

'No, indeed, and what would he be doing with a sword?' Quintilian asked rhetorically, and sat down.

'We'll get to the sword soon enough,' Blasus said dramatically, signaling for his next witness to come forward. This was the city guard who had come in response to the call for help from within the house. He described the scene he found there: the head of the family dead in his bed with a sword thrust deep into his chest, the weeping widow, the dazed and silent blind boy, the bloody hand prints in the corridor leading from the murder room to the boy's room.

'And what sort of sword was it that did the deed?' Blasus demanded.

'A regulation legionnaire's gladius. The short sword that is used by all the legions.'

'And do you have that sword with you?'

'I do.' The guard unrolled a bolt of red fabric he was carrying and revealed a plain, iron, double-edged sword, of the sort used by the regular infantry. The fore part of the blade was still crusted with the dried blood of Marcus Vexianus Abracius, and several of the jurors or audience members gasped at the sight. They had, most of them, performed military service for the State, and had seen men die before their eyes, and probably killed a few themselves. But there is a difference between battle and murder; one is sanctified by the gods, the other is a foul and cowardly act.

Blasus Parenas passed the sword around the jury and, eventually, even to the spectators. Finally, with a great sweeping gesture that fluttered his toga, he handed it to Quintilian. Then he turned back to the jury and, pacing from side to side in front of them with a deliberate gait, began his summation.

In the best tradition of the Roman prosecutor, Parenas went on for hours, and he had no trouble keeping the jurors awake. He began by drawing a word-portrait of the murdered Marcus; what a fine husband and father he had been, what a prince of an employer, what a noble Roman, with all the virtues that Rome looks for in her citizens.

And then on to the most important thing in a murder trial: motive. Unless the speaker can convince the jury that the defendant *wanted* to kill the victim, it's hard to convince them that he *did* kill the victim. And oh how Rufus Plenius wanted to kill his father, according to Blasus: 'And then a worm grew slowly inside of him; the worm of hate. He hated his father as the cause of his blindness; he hated his father because, in saving him first from the fire, he failed to save his beloved mother. Perhaps too beloved, but we'll let that pass.'

Blasus trotted out all the usual reasons why a son might murder his father, and added a few of his own: Rufus Plenius was angry that his father remarried, thus dishonoring his mother's memory. Rufus Plenius was secretly in love with his stepmother and jealous of his father. Marcus Vexianus Abracius had been a rich and successful man; Rufus Plenius was jealous of the success, and wanted to inherit his father's money and be free of his father's stifling influence. Free to do what, Blasus didn't say.

'And all of these,' Blasus intoned, 'finally came together in the disturbed mind of this poor boy one night a month ago when he took the sword that he had been hiding — possibly under his bed so he could reach down and feel the strength of the blade, the sharpness of the edge — and determined to strike, strike, strike! And cut down his father while the man slept — slept peacefully, expecting no harm, next to his loving wife.'

Now we were getting to it; the murder itself. The coughing and fidgeting among the jurors ceased, and they listened intently.

'Picture the scene,' Blasus told them. 'In the dead of night, the only time when a blind man can successfully hope to commit such a dastardly crime, Marcus's son leaves his room and creeps down the hall, sword in hand. He enters the bedroom where his father and stepmother are sleeping and — with one well-aimed thrust — stabs his father through the heart!' Here Blasus mimed a well-aimed thrust, and some in the audience shivered.

'And then young Rufus Plenius staggers back to his room, blindly leaving behind him the blood-red hand print of a murderer — not once but seven times — along the wall of the corridor.'

Blasus raised his hands to the heavens. 'Perhaps it was the gods that caused him to leave behind these bloody markers.' Blasus dropped his hands sadly to his sides. 'Perhaps, after his dreadful deed, the lad wanted to be caught. Who can say? But no one can deny his guilt — it is marked by his own hand on the corridor wall — and marked, and marked, and marked, and marked.' And Blasus sat down.

After a suitable pause Quintilian rose and faced the jury. 'Honorable Romans,' he began, 'I stand before you charged with the task of defending a young blind boy of impeccable character who has been accused of murder — and the most foul murder imaginable at that: the murder of his own father.

'I have heard speculation as to how I am going to plead this unfortunate lad's case.' Quintilian raised his right hand, palm upraised, in supplication to the jurors. 'I could beg for the court's mercy because the boy is blind and an orphan. I could attempt to convince you that he was driven mad with grief, and is therefore not responsible for his actions. I could speak to you of his heroism in saving his father from a terrible fire, and losing his eyesight in the attempt to save his mother. I could somehow try to justify this horrible crime.' He lowered his hand.

'But there is no justification for such a horrible crime. And, thanks to the gods who have opened my eyes to the truth, I do not have to attempt such a hopeless task. The fact is, as I will prove to you by the evidence we have already heard and about which there is no dispute, Rufus Plenius Abracius is innocent of the charge.' Quintilian moved over to stand next to his client, and put his hand on the boy's shoulder. 'He did not murder his father.'

There was a murmur from the jurors. The chairman of the court turned to glare them into silence, and then nodded at Quintilian to continue.

Quintilian gave the jurors a word picture of the life of Marcus Vexianus Abracius, his first wife and their son in the days before the fire, showing what a close and loving family they were. Then he spoke of Rufus Plenius's double tragedy of losing his mother and his eyesight. 'Even though it was not his fault,' Quintilian told them, 'the guilt and remorse he felt overwhelmed him. Yes he loved his mother, just as you and I love our mothers. We have no need to look to Oedipus for an explanation.' He looked slowly around at the jurors. 'Consider this my friends: How would you like to be on trial for something — anything, it doesn't matter what — and have some unctuous prosecutor tell the jury that your love for your mother was 'unnatural'? Bah! We will speak no more about it.'

Quintilian then verbally took the jurors along to watch sympathetically as Rufus Plenius retired to his room after the fire, to spend his days in darkness and in pain. Slowly he brought them along when Rufus Plenius suffered the new shock of his father's remarriage. 'Rufus Plenius was still clinging to the ghost of his mother,' he told them, 'when his father gave it up for a new love.' Rufus Plenius moved his bedroom further away from his father's so he would not have to listen to the endearments his father whispered to someone who was not his mother. But he didn't resent his father's new happiness, he merely didn't want to have to deal with it. 'A deceased wife,' Quintilian said, 'no matter how well loved, will make way in the mind for a new wife; replaced but not supplanted, the new love separate from the old. But a mother cannot be replaced.'

After a short pause, Quintilian continued, 'There is the vial of poison we have heard about. You all heard Serpo's description of Rufus Plenius's actions at his mother's tomb. Can any of you doubt that what was on his mind was suicide? Not the actions of an untroubled mind, perhaps, but hardly the equivalent of murder. We will speak no more about it.'

Now Quintilian reached down and picked up the sword Blasus had passed to him earlier and held it flat out before the jurors. 'We have been told this is the murder weapon, my friends. A good, honest Roman gladius. Perhaps it is, perhaps it

35

is. But if so, and if Rufus Plenius is the murderer, then where did he hide it before the murder? For he must have had it for a long time; he hadn't been away from his room except briefly for months. And those times he did leave his room, his faithful body slave Serpo went with him. Even when he didn't want Serpo along, even when he didn't know Serpo was following him, Serpo was there. But Serpo never saw Rufus Plenius with a sword. Did you, Serpo?' He looked out into the audience, where Serpo might be standing, and then looked back. 'And so blind Rufus Plenius must have hidden the sword, and he must have hidden it well.'

Quintilian suddenly raised the sword above his head with both hands. 'Close your eyes!' he commanded. 'All of you, close your eyes. Now you are blind — only for the moment, fortunately. Now you must go to someplace in your house, with family, servants and slaves all about, and hide a sword. Make sure no one sees you, even though you're blind and cannot tell who might be watching. Where will you put it? Under your bed, as Blasus would have it? And will the slave who makes up your bed not see it? And remember, at some future time you're going to have to come to this hiding place, wherever it is, and remove the weapon, in stealth and silence and unobserved. But are you unobserved? Can you be sure?'

Quintilian lowered the sword. I made a slight noise as I reached for a fresh tablet to continue taking down his words, and he looked crossly at me. Then he returned his gaze to the jurors. 'Let us look at the story of this crime as presented by my good friend Blasus Parenas,' he told them. 'He would have it that young Rufus Plenius rose from his bed in the middle of the night and retrieved the gladius from whatever secret location he had placed it unobserved. Then he crept down the corridor and opened the door to his father's room. Had his father been awake and cried, 'Why Rufus, what are you doing with that sword?' what would he have replied, do you suppose?

'And then perhaps the strangest act of all. Blind Rufus Plenius goes to his father's side and, with one unerring thrust, drives the point of the sword cleanly between the second and third rib and into his father's heart. There were no hesitation marks on the body, no secondary cuts, just the one clean thrust. How many among you, sighted men, trained soldiers many of you, could have done as well? Indeed this Rufus Plenius is a paragon.'

Quintilian lowered his voice dramatically and leaned forward. 'No, I was mistaken, there was one thing stranger — so strange indeed as to have been impossible. The bloody hand prints — the hand prints that were meant to convince all of my client's guilt, to secure his conviction before this court — could not have been created as we are supposed to believe they were created.

'The noble Blasus has left a picture in our minds of young Rufus, fresh from murdering his father, staggering back to his room and leaving a bloody hand print here, and a bloody hand print there, seven in all, as the unwitting signature of his guilt. But this was a corridor that Rufus Plenius was intimately familiar with; he walked it daily. He had no need

38

to feel his way along.' Quintilian pointed a lecturing finger at the jurors. 'Consider: would a man who, although blind, could thrust a sword cleanly between two ribs and into the heart have to feel his way along a familiar corridor?

'But, unlikely as it might be, I suppose it is possible. And I promised you a sight of the impossible. Well, you shall have it. Each of those prints on the corridor wall, as you have heard them described, as I myself have seen them, is from a hand freshly dipped in blood. It is a complete, whole, and damning print. But it does not damn Rufus Plenius Abracius. It is impossible for young Rufus to have made those prints. Blood does not behave that way.'

Quintilian paused and looked over his audience. 'Many of you are familiar, perhaps all too familiar, with the behavior of fresh blood. It would not stay on the hand to be impressed, time after time, to form a detailed image. The first one,' — he pressed his hand against an imaginary wall — 'would be clear. And perhaps the second. But by the third,'

— again his hand went up and pressed the air, and the jurors watched carefully — 'there would be less blood, and the print would be less distinct. And by the fourth, and fifth, and sixth, the print would diminish and diminish and diminish, until by the seventh it would be scarcely visible at all.'

He lowered his hand. 'No, my friends, those prints were made by someone who was unfamiliar with the action of blood. Someone who wanted Rufus Plenius to get the blame for her acts.' He turned to face the widow Lucilla. 'Yes, madam, I speak of you. For you murdered your own husband, and contrived for his son — his poor blind son — to get the blame. No one else could have, and no one else had the motive. Who helped you? Who procured the sword? Was it that handsome centurion that sits by your side? Has he been your lover while you were married to Marcus Vexianus Abracius, a tiresome old man twenty years your senior?'

The centurion leaped to his feet, his face red, and clutched the hilt of his sword.

Then he looked around and gulped and sat back down.

'Your motive, madam? Your stepson told me without knowing he did. When your husband dies you get only the widow's portion, and Rufus Plenius gets the rest — unless Rufus is found guilty of his father's murder and exiled or executed. Then he cannot inherit, and you get it all. So you had a double scheme all along: murder the father and blame the son.'

Lucilla stared stolidly at him across the rows of spectators and said nothing.

'And the sword, madam. Was he really killed with that sword? Or was it picked as a man's weapon, one that would not cause anyone to think of you? Did you kill him with a knife first? I rather think you did: a long, slender knife. And then you thrust the sword in the gaping wound; enlarging it so you could get enough blood to make those damning hand prints. And they are damning, madam, they truly are. For they are the prints of a small hand — the hand of Rufus Plenius, or the hand of Lucilla. And, as they were made on purpose to point to Rufus Plenius, we must assume they were made by Lucilla. What do you say, madam?'

She said nothing.

Quintilian turned back to the jurors. 'It is not my task here to prove this lady's guilt, only to establish my client's innocence. And I believe I have done that.'

And the voting bore him out. When the ballots were removed from the jar and counted, there were forty-six for innocent and only five for guilty.

The next day Titus came by to congratulate Quintilian and to see to his fee. 'Rufus Plenius will pay you when the estate is settled,' he told him. 'He has evicted that woman, but hasn't decided whether to prosecute her or not. Apparently the centurion, a young man from the northern provinces, was indeed her lover, although he has admitted nothing.'

'I assumed as much,' Quintilian said.

'How did you figure it out?'

'Yes,' I added, 'how?'

'Once I knew the lady was guilty, the pieces fell easily into place,' he told us.

'And how did you know that?' Titus asked.

'The hand prints were of her hand,' Quintilian said. 'When I looked closely at them I saw a slight curve in the print of the thumb. The lady had a scar on her thumb that matched the curve.'

'You did not mention that at the trial.'

'Of course not. Jurors don't like technical evidence, they will disagree with it as a matter of course. What they are swayed by is oratory: fine words strung together in telling sentences. That's what I teach, not peering at walls!'

'Oh,' Titus said.

'You are the master,' I told him, 'you really are.'

'You may write this case up,' Quintilian told me. 'I can use it as an example in my text book.'

'Yes, sir,' I said.

'But remember to stress the importance of the rhetoric,' he said. 'Not those little deductive details. They are not important.'

'Of course, sir,' I agreed.

2

Great Caesar's Ghost

It was on the Nones of September in the second year of the reign of Emperor Vespasian, many years ago now, that our involvement in the events that I am recounting here began. For reasons that will become clear as I continue my narrative, I could not record this at the time, as is my custom — as, indeed, is my task. As is, I fear, my excuse for being.

I am Plautus Maximilianus Aureus, a member of the household of the great orator and barrister Marcus Fabius Quintilianus and, as I describe myself, his perpetual student. Somewhat higher than a servant, and somewhat lower than a protégé, I earn my keep by taking down on wax tablets, in my own special shorthand, such speeches, comments, and ideas of Quintilian as are worth recording for use in the series of texts for the training of youth that Quintilian is writing, intends to write, or may someday get around to writing. When I am not attending my patron Quintilian, I transcribe my shorthand onto scraps of parchment or papyrus and organize the comments into a variety of different categories, such as: oratory, law, government, nature, music, human conduct, instruction for the young, instruction for those who would teach the young, and humor. The humor category is not overly crowded.

* * *

The fame of my patron as a barrister and rhetorician had been on the rise for the past few years, but I don't believe that even he had any idea just how high it had risen until that morning, when a squad of the Praetorian Guard appeared at the gate of Quintilian's villa. 'I would speak with Fabius Quintilianus the orator,' the decurion in charge told Peris, our gatekeeper.

Peris yawned and stretched, and tried to act as if having six men in bright, shiny armor appear at our gate was an everyday affair. 'It is barely past sunrise,' he told the decurion. 'I doubt whether my master is yet up.'

'I am on the emperor's business,' the decurion replied sternly. 'For me, he will arise.'

There was a time, and not so long ago, when having a squad of the emperor's Praetorian Guard appear at your front gate was a good reason for fleeing out the back gate, no matter how noble your family or how high your position. But the days of Caligula and Nero are in the past, and our present emperor is not known for intemperate rages or random murders. Still, the gods themselves have been known to fly into sudden fits over minor misunderstandings, so to my mind a sudden summons from Emperor Vespasian might not be cause for flight, but a little moment of sheer terror might be understandable.

The decurion told my mentor, who came grumbling to the door of his bedroom, that his orders were to take Quintilian directly to the emperor, and as quickly as possible. With that, Quintilian dressed, splashed some water on his face, threw a cloak on over his toga, and said, 'Lead on!'

I was already dressed, so I grabbed my sack of fresh wax tablets and fell in behind my mentor. I was so accustomed to accompanying Quintilian everywhere he went that we were halfway to the imperial palace before I realized that I had not been included in the summons, and Quintilian had not actually asked me to join him. Quintilian strode along, impatient with the measured tread of the guardsmen. I scurried to keep up; the sensation in my left leg, crippled from a childhood illness, progressing from a dull ache to a sharp, jarring pain with each step. But I have learned to live with pain.

The thoughts that were a great jumble in my head were of more concern than the pain in my leg, and I will admit they were unworthy of the lessons I have learned at the feet of the great Quintilian. If my mentor had somehow incurred the emperor's displeasure, would Vespasian throw him into a dungeon, or send him home to commit honorable suicide, or have him dispatched by the short sword of, perhaps, this very decurion that was taking us to the court? And, since I was with him, would the emperor include me in his displeasure, however expressed, as a matter of course?

★　★　★

We arrived at the east gate of the Golden House, the great palace that Nero had built (although he had died before it was finished, to the relief of all Rome), and were rushed through a series of rooms and courtyards, going deeper and deeper into the inner palace. At each doorway the decurion lifted his left hand, exposing to the guard a sigil he kept cupped in his palm, and announced, 'At the emperor's command!' And the guards stood aside as we hurried through. Shortly we reached what I assumed were the private living quarters of the emperor himself. There were guards scattered all through the vast structure, like golden raisins in a porridge, but here they were clustered closer together and they stood straighter, and their armor was even more highly polished.

The decurion handed us off to a gold-plated centurion, amid much saluting and foot-stomping, and the centurion clasped hands with Quintilian. 'They call me Sabatinus,' the centurion told him. 'I am to take you directly to the emperor.'

'Do you know what this is about?' Quintilian asked.

'Not a clue. Have you met Vespasian before?'

'Once, briefly. A ceremonial occasion.'

'Then for your information: he dislikes being called 'emperor,' or 'Caesar,' or 'princeps,' or any of the other titles he has to use in public. Call him 'General Vespasian,' or just 'General.''

Centurion Sabatinus took us through a great hall and we entered a corridor wide enough for a goods wagon to pass along without scraping the sides and long enough to require a lusty shout to be heard at the far end. Not that I attempted a lusty shout — that was just my impression. There were a pair of great bronze doors a comfortable distance along the corridor, flanked by two glittering guardsmen, but the centurion skirted by them and took us instead to a small black door near the corridor's end. The guardsman at the door intoned, 'They are both in there,' under his breath, and pulled it open.

We entered. The room was small, plainly furnished with a flat board for a desk, several camp chairs, and a nest of cubbyholes along one wall filled with scrolls and rolled documents of various sorts. And *they* were indeed in the room. Sitting behind the flat board of a desk, bent over a lengthy scroll, his body squat and hard, his face the square, blunt, honest face admired by his legionaries, was Titus Flavius Vespasianus, subduer of the Britains under Emperor Claudius; conqueror of the Jews under Emperor Nero; and now himself Emperor of Rome and sole ruler of the Roman Empire, which encompassed most of the known world. Standing by his side, holding a partially unrolled scroll, was his twenty-year-old son Domitian, Titus Flavius Domitianus, who had been his father's presence in Rome while his father was in Judea, and was now Vespasian's trusted right hand.

I looked over Domitian carefully, for I

had heard much about him. He was young; younger even than I. He was handsome, with a square jaw and a shock of dark, curly hair. His feelings, whatever they might be, were reserved and did not show on his face, which was a mask on which a slight, disdainful smile was the only visible emotion.

Some say Domitian was jealous of his brother's success. Vespasian's older son Titus had been left behind in Judea to finish the job of subduing the Jews, and had taken and sacked their capital city of Jerusalem and burned their temple the year before, ending once and for all the incessant bothersome revolts of these religious zealots with their 'Our god is better than any of your gods' fanaticism.

Some of those who claimed to have an ear into what happened inside the palace walls, those who studied the currents within the imperial household with the diligence of nervous lovers interpreting their beloved's every sigh and gesture, said with a sneer that Domitian was just as glad not to be facing the rigors — and dangers — of a martial campaign.

There are many who seem to know, and will be glad to whisper to you in great detail, the secrets of the palace; yet I have observed that those who actually do know seldom can be persuaded to speak. That last sentence has a nice flow. I believe I have just written an aphorism of some worth. I would read it aloud to Quintilian, but he would assuredly first compliment me on it and then spend some time telling me how to improve it. And most galling of all: he would be right. I think I shall not show it to him at this time.

★ ★ ★

The centurion came to attention by Vespasian's desk. 'Marcus Fabius Quintilianus, as directed, General.'

Vespasian looked up. 'Ah!' Then he turned to look at me, and I believe I turned white with fright. 'And who is this?'

Quintilian stared at me, I swear by Janus, as though he had never seen me before. 'My scribe Plautus, General,' he said finally.

'A scribe, eh?'

'I also use him as my personal assistant,' Quintilian added.

'I see.' Vespasian glared at me. 'You may assist the honorable Quintilian, if he needs your assistance,' he told me sternly. 'But you are not to scribe a single word of what transpires here. Is that clear?'

'Yes, your, ah, general,' I managed to get out.

'Good.' Vespasian made a gesture, and the centurion saluted and left the room. 'I have a problem,' the emperor of all the known world told Quintilian, lacing his hands behind his head, leaning back in his chair, and staring at Quintilian through half-closed eyes, 'and, from all I have heard of you, I am depending on you to discover the solution for me. Pull over one of those camp chairs, and enlighten my son and me with your wisdom.' He spoke in a measured voice, as though each word were weighed before it was uttered. I suppose that if I knew that my every word would be dissected, parsed, examined and discussed by a sycophantic, back-stabbing collection of Roman courtiers, I, too, would get into the habit of speaking with great care.

Quintilian moved one of the leather-covered camp chairs over to the desk and sat. I squatted on the floor next to him and restrained myself from pulling a wax tablet from my bag.

'I thank you for your faith in my judgment,' my master said, 'but I'm not sure I should thank whoever passed on such a glowing account of my small abilities. I am a rhetorician, with some success in pleading cases before the courts of Rome. If it is skill with words you require, I shall be honored to write speeches for you, as Seneca is said to have done for Nero. But I know nothing of statecraft, or of warfare, or of the numerous intrigues that doubtless cloud the imperial court.'

'And yet when I ask the courtiers who infest this place to find me the wisest man in Rome, those who did not immediately drop to the floor and chant 'You are, oh mighty Caesar,' seemed to think that, since Seneca died, it is probably one Marcus Fabius Quintilianus. I also had my staff ask of various learned men whom they would recommend for solving an arcane problem, and your name was mentioned frequently.'

Quintilian smiled a thin smile. 'These must not have been friends of mine, General,' he said. 'My friends would have assured you of my almost invincible stupidity.'

'He is the one!' Domitian interrupted, leaning forward, his knuckles on the desk. 'I told you, father, what the Sybil said.' He turned to Quintilian. 'My father and I have chosen you for this task. You are expected to comply!'

Vespasian raised a hand. 'I apologize for my son,' he said. 'He has not yet learned that there are some people to whom you must give orders, and others from whom you may request, but not require, assistance. If you do not feel you are fit for the task, it would waste both of our time for you to attempt it.'

Domitian swallowed and sat down by the side of the desk.

'And just what is the task, General?' Quintilian asked.

'People here in the palace; guards, courtiers, and others, recount that they have been seeing a ghost wandering about these halls. Or so they say. I want you to find out just what it is they are seeing and, if it is a ghost, convince it to go away. And, for that matter, if it isn't a ghost, convince it to go away.'

'A ghost?'

'Just so,' Vespasian said, looking annoyed. 'And not just any ghost. The shade, to be precise, of Gaius Julius Caesar.'

I stifled an exclamation.

'Julius Caesar? He's been with his fellow gods for over a century now,' Quintilian said.

'A hundred and twelve years,' Vespasian affirmed. 'Why, you may ask, if he were to come back, would he return to Nero's palace; a place he'd never seen in his life built by a man he'd most assuredly despise? I have no answer. But that doesn't stop him from walking these halls, at least according to those who have seen him.'

Quintilian nodded. 'Reports of ghosts should be taken seriously,' he said. 'But would it not be better to get Pliny the naturalist to investigate this? I understand he's writing some sort of vast book on these sorts of natural phenomena.'

'We sent someone to ask his advice,' Domitian said. 'He's at his estate in Como. He recommended you.'

'Ah!' My master nodded thoughtfully. 'And just what was it that the Sybil said?'

Vespasian sighed. 'My son went to Cumae to consult the Sybil about two weeks ago. He asked my permission, and I complied. I thought a favorable prediction would end the mutterings.'

'The mutterings?'

Vespasian made a gesture to his son, who took up the story. 'A figure wearing a senatorial toga with a laurel wreath circling his head has been seen wandering throughout this building at all times of the day and night — but mostly at night. He disappears when anyone attempts to approach. Those who have seen him report that he looks like the busts of Julius Caesar. I think every Roman has a good idea of what the great Caesar looked like.'

'Even so,' Quintilian agreed.

'Some even report seeing open wounds on the figure, such as Caesar received on that fateful Ides of March,' Domitian continued. 'And the blood dripping on the ground. But no blood has been found when the area was examined.'

'I see,' Quintilian said. 'So we have a disappearing specter who looks like great Caesar. How long has this been going on?'

'At least two months. Perhaps longer.'

'Have either of you ever seen it?'

Vespasian shook his head. His son said, 'No, we have not been so fortunate.'

'So. And why are the ruler of the Roman Empire and his son so concerned about this specter flitting about the palace that they feel the need to ask for my poor services?'

'Two things,' Vespasian said. 'First, the shade has begun to speak.'

'Speak?'

Domitian stood up and leaned over the desk. '"Beware the Ides of October,"' he recited. 'That's what the fool thing has started to say. Bah! If it *was* Caesar, it'd probably be saying 'Where are the girls,' or more likely, 'Where are the boys?''

'Now, son.' Vespasian fixed his younger

son with a stony glare. 'Those are vile calumnies spread by Caesar's enemies when he had joined the gods and was no longer around to defend himself. Jove only knows what they'll be saying about me when I, ah, ascend.'

'Beware the Ides of October,' Quintilian repeated. 'Not good.'

'No.' Vespasian grimaced. 'And you know how superstitious the average Roman is; always looking for portents and appealing for help from one god or another. When I embark on a campaign I must have the legion's soothsayer inspect the entrails of a pigeon and a rabbit to make sure the signs are favorable. My troops might refuse to move if I did not.'

Something about Vespasian's glare as he said that told me that the soothsayer knew in advance just what he'd better find in those entrails.

'It makes me a prisoner in this blasted palace of Nero's,' Vespasian continued. 'I want to move out. I *planned* to move out. This gilded claptrap is too ornate — too Nero — for me. Now that it's finally finished, I plan to turn it into an imperial forum, or a series of temples to the more important gods, or something. I plan to build myself a simple — well, comparatively simple — imperial abode by the Field of Mars. But I cannot move with this specter hanging over me. I cannot seem to be moving from fear. If I leave while this is going on, my troops will lose respect for me. And there are still followers of Otho or Vitellius about who would just as soon see me dead. And if that happens we'll have another year with three or four emperors, one after the other, bim, bam, like that, fighting to stay in power. And Rome couldn't stand it.'

'So the ghost of Julius Caesar is keeping you in Nero's palace by threatening your death. I assume that's how you interpret the 'Ides of October' business?'

Vespasian shrugged his broad shoulders. 'How else?'

Quintilian nodded. 'And that's why your son consulted the Sybil?'

'It was right after I first heard of the 'Ides of October,'' Domitian said. 'I went to Cumae with a small bodyguard, and paid the priests for an audience with the

Sybil. I did not tell them who I was.'

Sure, I thought, *just some random nobleman guarded by a troop of the Praetorian Guard.* But I kept my mouth shut.

Domitian continued, 'The priests kept me waiting for most of the day. Then, as dusk fell, I was taken into the cave. 'Sybil,' the priest said, 'this is Vergilus,' for such is what I had told them was my name.'

'What did the Sybil look like?' Quintilian asked.

'The cave was dark, and lit by torches, and it was difficult to tell,' Domitian said. 'One moment she looked young and beautiful — unbelievably beautiful — with long, dark hair, and a slender, sinuous body. And the next moment she looked old, unbelievably old, and wise beyond the knowledge of mortal men.'

'Ah!' Quintilian said, running his forefinger along the side of his nose. 'Tell me, did you smell anything?'

Domitian thought for a moment. 'Some kind of incense. Perhaps it was from the smoke coming from a vent in the rock. It made my head spin.'

'Ah!' Quintilian said again.

'She looked at me for a long moment. And then she said to me, 'Hail, ruler of men.'

''I am no ruler of men,' I told her.

''You are what I say you are,' she said. 'You have come about a Caesar,' she said, 'the Caesar that is yet to be concerned about the Caesar that was.''

'Indeed?' Quintilian said.

Domitian nodded. 'I was startled. I am no fool; I know the priests could have guessed who I was from my raiment, or from the guards I traveled with. But I told no man the purpose of my quest.'

'And what was it she told you?'

'She seemed to go into a trance. For a long while she said nothing. Finally she said, she sort of chanted,

''*The past returns through the wiles of men*
It is not hard to die
Saying does not make it so
The highly regarded ignorant one will cleave the knot
And Caesar shall create a school in his answer.''

'This verse,' Quintilian asked, 'is it precisely what she said?'

Domitian nodded. 'A priest sort of hides in a corner and writes down everything she says. He wrote out a copy for me.'

'I don't know what else it may mean,' Vespasian said, 'but you are marked by your own words. It is clear that you are the highly regarded ignorant one who will cleave the knot.'

Quintilian thought for a moment and then looked up. 'You said there were two things.'

'I did.' Vespasian turned to his son. 'Domitian, show our learned friend the other, ah, thing.'

'Very well.' Domitian stood up and gestured for us to accompany him. We went a short way down the corridor and entered a short separate hallway leading to a single door. A guardsman before the door stiffened into a living statue of The Perfect Guardsman At Attention at our approach.

'At ease, guardsman,' Domitian said. 'Has anything happened during your watch? Anything at all?'

'No, sir,' the guardsman spat out between clenched teeth, his face turning red from the effort of talking without moving his lips.

'Thank you. Remain at ease.' Domitian pushed open the door. 'This is — was — the anteroom to Nero's throne room,' he told us. 'My father chooses not to use a throne room, but has a small audience chamber in another part of the palace.'

★　★　★

The anteroom was small, the walls decorated with a continuous painted scene of woodland beauty, including several scantily-clad nymphs darting among the trees. There were two doors: the door we had come in, and a door across the room leading to the throne room. Whatever furnishings the chamber had held during Nero's time had been removed. It was now bare, except for one, lone, corpse lying in a grotesque heap in the middle of the floor.

'He was found early this morning,' Domitian said. 'The throne room is occupied through the night. It is used as the guardroom for posting the night guards. The hallway is under guard all night. Nobody saw the lad go in or out. And yet, here he is.'

The corpse was a young man in a white tunic and sandals; by his dress not a slave, but not a high-status Roman either. Possibly a freedman servant. He had been stabbed several times in the chest and neck. There was surprisingly little blood, but the victim had apparently used what there was to draw the number XIII on the floor above his head with his right forefinger as he was dying.

'Thirteen,' Quintilian said.

'The Ides of October fall on the thirteenth,' Domitian said.

'Yes,' my mentor agreed. 'That would be it, of course. Who is the dead lad?'

'One of the pages. Name was, I believe, Septius.'

'What were his duties?'

'I have no idea. You can ask.'

'Who saw him last, that is, when he was alive?'

'You may ask that, too.'

Vespasian appeared in the doorway behind us. 'Well?' he asked.

Quintilian turned to him. 'This lad was not killed by a ghost,' he said.

Vespasian sighed. 'You know that, citizen Quintilian, and I know that. But when word of this gets out, it will be hard to convince the mob. Including, I am afraid, most of my guardsmen.'

'All right, General. I will try to resolve this ghostly business for you. After all, we cannot make a liar of the Sybil. First I must spend some time examining this poor lad's body. Then I must see the various places where this apparition has appeared. And then I will speak with all those who claim to have seen Caesar's ghost, and particularly those who have heard it speak.'

'Yes,' Vespasian agreed. 'And I must find out who the lad's parents are. They must be notified. Death is always cruel and often unnecessary, even in battle. This' — he gestured at the body — 'this is a waste.' He looked down at the corpse and shook his head. 'I sometimes think that the only death that is not difficult to accept is your own.'

'It is not hard to die,' Quintilian said.

We all looked at him. 'It is not hard to die,' he repeated. 'That's what the Sybil said.'

'So it is,' Vespasian remembered.

'When Nero was escaping the mob he hid himself in this palace for a day and pleaded with the head of his guards, to save him. The guard declined, saying, 'Is it so hard, then, to die?' which is a line from one of Virgil's plays, I believe. Upon which, Nero fled to the countryside.'

'The theater does not interest me,' Vespasian said.

'But it might explain the Sybil's quote,' Domitian offered.

'How?'

'I don't know yet,' Quintilian said. 'Give me some time.'

★   ★   ★

Vespasian and Domitian left us alone in the room. Domitian said that he would arrange for the centurion to be waiting outside for us when we were ready.

Quintilian examined the corpse slowly and carefully, from head to foot, taking an oil lamp from its fixture on the wall to give himself better light. I watched as best I could, but I confess I am not yet hardened to the sight of dead bodies. 'Notice how little blood there is,' he commented.

'Indeed,' I agreed.

He rolled the body over. 'The back is completely clear of wounds, and of blood. The boy was attacked only from the front.'

'Even so,' I agreed.

'He has a small sheath here on his belt,' Quintilian commented, 'but the knife is missing.'

'Perhaps he was killed by his own knife,' I suggested.

'Perhaps,' Quintilian said, 'but I think a larger weapon was used, judging by the size of the wounds. I would that you could take notes, but as that is forbidden, try to remember what you see and what I tell you.'

'Yes, mentor,' I said. 'I will do my best.'

'The boy was not killed here,' Quintilian said. 'He died elsewhere, and was carried

68

here. If he had been stabbed repeatedly here, the strokes of the knife would have splattered blood over the floor and walls.'

'But both entrances were watched.'

'No one was assigned the task of actually watching the entrances to this room,' Quintilian said. 'Besides, he came here somehow, alive or dead, despite the possible watchers.'

'True,' I said.

Quintilian went to the door and opened it. The young centurion was waiting patiently outside with two guardsmen, who snapped to attention when they saw Quintilian emerge. My master was, if only for the moment, a person of some stature in the palace. 'Sabatinus,' Quintilian called.

The centurion came over to the door and looked curiously at the body lying inside.

'Did you know about this?' Quintilian asked, indicating the corpse.

'Oh, yes,' Sabatinus said. 'News travels fast within the palace walls. There are, I believe, few secrets.'

'I assume no bloody room has been

noticed about the palace this morning?'

Sabatinus thought for a second. 'It could be that some of the servants found such a room, and thought to clean it up without mentioning it to anyone. I will have enquiries made.'

'Also there is a small knife missing from the dead lad's sheath. See if anyone found it.'

'I didn't notice the missing knife. I shall have a search made.'

We left the room and closed the door behind us. 'Do you know of the ghost said to be wandering these corridors?' Quintilian asked the centurion.

'Great Caesar's ghost? Yes, I have heard tell.'

'But you have never seen it yourself?'

'No.'

'What do you think of the stories?'

Sabatinus thought for a moment. 'I thought it was an amusing thing for us to have our own personal ghost — and that of Great Caesar, at that. But when it was reported that the specter had begun to speak, then I began to wonder if it might have greater portent.'

'Then you believe the stories?'

'No, in truth I can't say I believe them.' Sabatinus smiled. 'But were I to come face-to-face with this specter, I might rapidly change my opinion.'

Quintilian nodded. 'Can you gather the people who claim to have actually seen this wraith and send them in to speak with me?'

'I will make a list of names, and then send some of my guardsmen in search of the people you require.'

'Fine. Let not status be considered in your search. From slave to senator; if the person claims to have seen the specter, I would like to speak with him — or her.'

'Very good. It will take some time.'

'Also bring me whoever saw this page last when he was alive, and someone who knows what he was supposed to be doing at the time. They may well be the same person.'

'Very good. I will put some men on it.'

'Find me a suitable room in which to wait, provided with chairs, a desk of some sort if possible, and refreshments. We have not yet eaten this morning.'

71

'It shall be as you wish.'

'And tell — whoever — to remove that poor young man's body.'

'And clean the blood from the floor. That, also, shall be done.'

*   *   *

Centurion Sabatinus showed us to a room about the size of a large bedroom. It was lit by a skylight, and had wide benches strewn with cushions around three of the walls. What it had originally been intended for, I have no idea. After a few minutes a couple of guardsmen brought in a slab-top desk, much like the one Vespasian had been working on, and several folding chairs. And some time after that two serving girls came in bearing trays of food: dried fish and several sorts of olives and bread and olive oil and little pastries filled with lentils and spinach and figs and slices of melon, and a pitcher of a good Falernian wine. My master was hungry. He ate. After a moment he pushed a plate my way. I was hungry. I ate.

'How do you suppose,' I asked my mentor, who was staring thoughtfully at a fig, 'the Sybil knows what she knows?'

Quintilian turned to stare thoughtfully at me. 'What, exactly, does she know?' he asked.

'I don't know,' I said.

'Neither do I.' He ate the fig.

The first witness was brought in shortly after that. A short, round man who worked in the kitchens, he was very nervous and kept fiddling with his white cap, dropping it several times during the brief interview.

'Your name?' Quintilian asked.

'Osterius, if it please your excellency.'

'Relax, Osterius; you have been brought here merely to tell us what you saw.'

'About the ghost, your excellency?'

'Just so. About the ghost.'

'I didn't see nothing I shouldn't have seen, your excellency.' He dropped his cap and bent over, trying to snare it without looking down.

'Of course not,' Quintilian said, waiting patiently for him to retrieve the cap. 'But, just what did you see?'

'It wasn't my fault. I didn't want to see

it. It was just there.'

'Yes. Where?'

'What?'

'Where did you see it? Where were you when you saw it?'

'In the storeroom sir, where we keep the jars of pickled foodstuffs.'

'Ah. You saw it in the storeroom?'

'Well, I was like in the storeroom. The ghost was outside, in the corridor.'

Quintilian nodded and smiled an encouraging smile. 'Very good. You're very observant. What was it doing?'

'Eating, sir. A chicken leg, I think.'

'And then what happened?'

'Well, he saw me about when I saw him. He looked just like the great Julius Caesar looked on some of them old coins, and on the busts in the Forum. And he looked kind of — ghostly. He kind of smiled, and waved at me. And then he went around the corner. But when Scullius and me went around the corner — he was gone.'

'Scullius?'

'Yes, your honor. My mate who was waiting for me in the small preparation room.'

'So you didn't go right after this ghost?'

'No way, your excellency. I went to get Scullius first. Then the two of us, we went back and followed him around the corner. And he was gone. And there wasn't no place for him to go. The only room around that corner is locked with a special lock, to which only the wine master has the key, 'cause it contains the amphorae of Greek wine what come in special wagons from way up North.'

'Ah!' Quintilian said. 'When was this?'

Osterius thought for a moment. 'About six weeks ago.'

'Did you ever see the ghost again?'

'No, sir. Once were enough.'

'Indeed. Thank you for your help.'

Osterius was our interviewee number I, and his story was not that different from numbers II, III, IV or V. Man or woman sees figure who looks like what they imagine Julius Caesar to look like standing in some place where no human ought to be standing — down an empty corridor, or sitting on a bench in a closed courtyard, or at the far end of a deserted room; and they stay frozen in astonishment, or sheer fright, while the figure ambles out of sight, often going into some area from which there is no exit, and disappears.

Number VI, a stocky overseer named Lipato, had the first real variant to the usual story. 'It was about two weeks ago,' he told my master, helping himself to one of the smoked sprats that were heaped on the food tray. 'We were in the third courtyard, which has been turned into a garden, planting some flowers, or I think maybe vines of some sort. It was at night because the gardener says that these particular horticultures has got to be planted at night to grow right. Then I hears it.'

'What?'

'This voice. High and squeaky, it was. 'Vespasian,' it says. Beg pardon, and I hope his mightiness the emperor will forgive me, but that's what it says. 'Vespasian — oh woe onto you Vespasian! Beware the Ides of October,' it says. Fairly scared me so much I couldn't eat my breakfast.'

'And did you see anything to connect with this voice?'

'Oh, yes. Otherwise it might have been like a joke, you know. But there he was, standing there, as clear as daylight. Julius Caesar himself, in the flesh. Well, maybe not the flesh, but in the whatever-he-was-in. Big nose, laurel wreath around his head, and everything. His toga looked kind of loose and flappy, like maybe there wasn't too much flesh under it.'

'This was at night?'

'Yes, but we had maybe a dozen torches stuck in the ground all around — so the slaves could see what they were planting, after all.'

'So it was you and some slaves — '

'That's right. Maybe half a dozen slaves. And Master Funitus, the assistant to the chief assistant head gardener.'

'And you all saw and heard this?'

'Indeed.'

'And you didn't run after this apparition and try to grab it?'

'Couldn't.'

'You couldn't?'

'That's right. It was on the balcony, which runs around the courtyard. And by the time Master Funitus yelled something — he claims he yelled, 'Let's get it,' but it sounded more to me like, 'Let's get out of here.' Anyways, when he yelled, the thing, whatever it was, took a step backwards, gave out with another squeaky, 'Beware the Ides of October!' and disappeared.'

Quintilian leaned back in his chair and stared across the desk at the stocky foreman. 'I take it that you were not overly impressed with this phantom. Don't you believe in ghosts?'

Lipato shrugged. 'Might have been a ghost, might not. At any rate, it wasn't any danger to me, nor was it going to do me any good, as I saw it. Anyway, if it was a ghost, and it wanted to talk to the emperor, why didn't it just flit through a couple of walls and do it properly? It don't make sense.'

'The ways of the spirit world are beyond human understanding,' Quintilian said. 'Or so I've always heard.'

'It did put the fear of the gods in the slaves that were in the garden, I'll tell you that,' Lipato said.

Lipato left and was replaced by a slim young man who, by the drape of his toga and the inclination of his chin, proclaimed himself to be from an old and noble family.

His bearing and attitude filled me with an instant dislike, but the feeling was as instantly dispelled by his first words.

'You're the famous Marcus Fabius Quintilianus,' he said, with a sweeping bow. 'I am the orator Aopilis Romulus Laius, and I tremble with delight to meet you.'

'Tremble with delight?' Quintilian asked, looking slightly startled.

'It is a Greek pleasantry,' Laius said. 'Perhaps a bit effulgent when translated into Latin, but the emotion is sincere. I teach oratory and rhetoric and whenever I hear that you are going to speak, in a trial or a public debate, I hasten to be in the audience so that I may learn from the master.'

Quintilian frowned, but I think it was to disguise a pleased smile. 'You have a school here in Rome?' he asked.

'Not precisely a school,' Laius said. 'I do not teach children. My efforts are directed toward those adults who would improve their Latin, their deportment, and their rhetorical skills to enable them to better fit in with their, ah, new-found place in society.'

'Ah, I see,' Quintilian said, and he did smile. 'You teach the newly rich to, as some would put it, ape their betters.'

'Some might put it that way,' Laius said defensively. 'It is true that my students are, for the most part, freedmen and former slaves who have succeeded in making their fortunes in trade, or other occupations frowned upon by the patrician landowners. But some of those same landowners . . . well, never mind; I'm sure you don't want to hear my protests about the social order.'

'Perhaps some other time,' Quintilian said. 'Right now I'm more interested in ghosts.'

'Yes, of course. That's why I'm here.' Laius hitched up his toga and sat down. 'I saw this supposed ghost, it would be, four days ago. Here in the palace.'

'Just when and where, if you can remember.'

'Remember? How could I forget? I was waiting in a courtyard — I'm not sure just which courtyard, there are so many of them in this place, but I could find it again if you like — when this person appeared in the middle of a tree about twelve feet off the ground.'

'A tree?' I exclaimed.

They both looked at me. 'It turns out that it was a potted tree,' Laius explained, 'and the pot had been moved so that it concealed a balcony. The person was on this balcony. 'Vespasian,' he said, 'Vespasian, beware the Ides of October! Mind what I say!' And then he screeched, and stepped backwards until he was out of sight.'

'Your description,' Quintilian said, 'makes it sound as though you do not believe the person was a ghost. Is this so?'

The teacher of oratory thought for a moment and then nodded. 'I am being cautious about calling it a ghost, because I do not think it was a ghost,' he admitted. 'Although the three or four other people in the courtyard at the time seemed to have no such doubts. They trembled and fell on their knees, and one of them went screaming out the entrance. But for me, I saw nothing ghostly about the figure. True, it did resemble Gaius Julius Caesar, but my uncle Timidus bears an uncanny resemblance to the god Bacchus, as may be seen by comparing him to many a mural in the various houses of joy about the city.'

'I see.'

'And besides, the person spoke with the slight hint of a foreign accent.'

'Really? You are the first to note that.'

'Most people wouldn't. You see, the problem was that his Latin was a hair too perfect, as though it had been learned as an adult. Much like some of the people I teach.'

'So you couldn't say what sort of accent?'

Laius shook his head. 'From the East, rather than the North, I would say; but aside from that, no.'

Quintilian nodded. 'Thank you, citizen Laius. One last question: What were you doing in that courtyard?'

'Waiting to see the imperial procurator. My father's estates were confiscated by Nero, and I am engaged in a continuing struggle to get them back.'

'With what luck?'

'None — absolutely none. It matters

not that most of the policies of Nero have been rescinded. In matters of property, the government is most reluctant to retrace its steps. I suppose they're afraid to open the box. I mean, if an estate grabbed by Nero is returned, then what about one confiscated by Claudius, or even Augustus?'

'There is something in what you say. But, if it is so hopeless, then why do you keep trying?'

'It gives me an air of moral authority among my patrons. Knowing that there's a chance, however small, that I may one day once again be as rich as they are causes them to treat me with ever-so-slightly more respect than they would otherwise.'

'Thank you again, citizen Laius.'

'Have I been of some help?'

'You have added to our store of information, and that is always helpful.'

★ ★ ★

Our next guest was a senator, Marius Trabitus by name. Sort of round, but none the less solidly built, and definitely past middle age, he had sharp eyes and a crisp, yet measured way of speaking, as though no words passed his lips until he had examined them carefully to make sure they conveyed just what he wanted them to convey, and no more. 'Glad to be of help,' he said, his eyes taking in the room, with more than one glance toward the platters of food on the table. 'Glad to be of help. You want me to tell you about my encounter with the shade of Julius Caesar?'

'Yes, Senator. If you please.'

'It was frightening, frightening,' Trabitus said, sitting down across from my master and helping himself to a couple of dates from the platter. 'It happened about a week ago now. It was late, quite late. I was in the anteroom to General Vespasian's audience chamber — the general dislikes calling it a throne room, and indeed he has no throne in the room — waiting to speak with the general, when suddenly he appeared before me. Just — appeared — like that — ' He waved a pudgy hand through the air to show what it was like.

'Who?'

'Why, Great Caesar's ghost, that's who. One second the room was empty, and the next, there he was. 'Vespasianus,' he called, 'beware the Ides of October.' And he sighed mightily, and dripped blood from gaping wounds in his toga. He stared at me, and I stared at him. I thought of trying to go and touch him, but I seemed to be rooted to the floor. I did not feel fear, but a sort of tremendous awe, as though I were in the presence of something greater than a mere mortal. And then all at once he disappeared, like blowing out a candle. And — you won't believe this — when I went to look, there was no blood on the floor! It was then that I felt fear. And then, like an echo from beyond, came the words again, 'Beware the Ides of October!''

Quintilian leaned forward. 'And what did you do?'

'I just stood there. I mean, after all what could I do?'

Quintilian nodded. 'What, indeed?'

'Shortly thereafter a page came for me to take me in to speak with General Vespasian, and I told him what had transpired.'

'The page or General Vespasian?'

'Both, I'm afraid. And probably everyone else I saw for the next few days. I tell you, it quite unnerved me.'

'I can believe that. And what did you make of it?'

'What did I make of it?'

'Yes. What do you think it meant?'

Trabitus looked as if he were about to say something, and then thought better of it. 'I don't know,' he said finally. 'I mean — it's not for me to say.'

Quintilian nodded. 'Yes,' he said. 'Very wise. You just report what has happened; let others mull over its possible meaning.'

Trabitus stood up and took one last fig. 'I heard about the young lad who was killed,' he said, shaking his head. 'A small knife is of no use against a ghost.' He ate the fig. 'I suppose a large knife wouldn't be much help, either.'

'I think certain sorts of incense and the reciting of the proper prayers are usually regarded as efficacious,' Quintilian said. 'But there is a lack of general agreement on just which sorts of incense and which prayers to use.'

Trabitus looked dubious. 'I suppose you're right,' he said. 'I hope I've been of some help.'

'I believe you have,' Quintilian told him. Trabitus glided from the room, and Quintilian turned to look at me.

'Yes?' I asked.

He put his knuckle to his lips and stared off into space, working on the phrasing of what he was about to tell me; I recognized the signs. 'When the improbable passes over into the impossible, the wall of truth has been breached,' he said.

'I can't write it down,' I told him. 'Very nice, whatever it means, but I can't write it down.'

'But it doesn't have . . . yes, I suppose you're right. See if you can remember it to include it in my collection of aphorisms for the young.'

'Yes, sir,' I told him.

Our next guest stomped in and declared, 'Decurion Carlus to see Investigator Quintilian as directed!' and then came to attention, standing as rigid as a marble column before the makeshift desk. He was a big man — not tall, but big in every other dimension. His arms were as big around as a wrestler's thighs. It would take two normal men with their arms outstretched to encompass his chest. His neck was so thick that his head seemed to emerge from it instead of being supported by it. His nose was flat, his ears were small and hugged the side of his head, and an ancient scar that ran from his chin to his right temple made his face look lopsided.

'Sit down, Decurion Carlus,' my master said, gesturing toward the chair Carlus stood next to.

The massive decurion lowered himself gingerly into the chair. 'I am here about the lad who got killed last night,' he said.

'Septius?' Quintilian asked.

'That was his name, yes.'

'Do you know how he died?'

'I do not, unfortunately. He was a good lad. Wanted to be a legionary. Would have made a good one, too; intelligent, cool-headed, took orders well. The last I saw of him, he was chasing a ghost.' A plain, matter-of-fact statement, with no more emotion behind it than if he'd said,

'The last time I saw him he was eating a fig.'

'Ah,' Quintilian said. 'When and where was this?'

'At the start of second watch. I had assembled the guards to post them — relieving the first watch, you know — when a figure that looked a lot like Julius Caesar, from the busts and coins and such, you know, appeared above us — '

'Above you?'

'On this sort of balcony. Our guard room was Nero's music room, or some such, and there's this small balcony sticking out of one wall. Well, this apparition, or whatever, starts yelling about the Ides of October, or some such. I pay it little attention, as I have to get my men posted. And besides, the way I figure it, if I act like it don't mean anything, why then the lads won't take it seriously. They'll think it's some sort of joke, like. Otherwise, if they take it serious, well, it could mean trouble. Most of the lads are from the northern provinces, and they're a superstitious lot.'

'You don't believe in ghosts?'

'I don't know about that,' Carlus said. 'But I don't believe they've got any business interfering with my men, when I'm trying to get them posted for guard duty.'

'A sensible attitude,' Quintilian said, nodding.

'Well, I give the men an 'eyes forward,' and start marching them to their posts, when young Septius, who was in there repairing some lacings on his sandals, suddenly jumps up and says, 'That ain't no ghost! I'll see about that!' and goes racing out of the room. I don't know what got into him. Maybe he saw something that I didn't.'

'That could be. Do you know where he went?'

'He was heading toward the stairs to the balcony when last I saw him. When I got back from posting the guard, he was gone, and I didn't hear any more about him until somebody came in this morning and said they'd found him dead.'

'What did you think?'

'I didn't think it was no ghost. What use would a ghost have in stabbing a man to death? Not the way of ghosts at all, from what I hear.'

Quintilian smiled. 'What use, indeed,' he said. 'You've been a big help, and I thank you.'

'A nice lad,' Carlus said. 'Sorry about whatever happened to him. You bring that ghost forward and my lads and I will take care of him good.'

'I'll try to do just that,' Quintilian told him.

* * *

We saw several more people in the next hour or so, but they added nothing to what we already knew. Of course, as far as I could see, what we already knew added nothing to what we already knew. On reviewing that sentence I can see that it makes little sense, and Quintilian would chastise me for writing it and tell me to write, clearly and concisely, exactly what I mean. What I mean is that we had interviewed over a dozen people, and learned that the ghost of Julius Caesar appeared at times, gave a doleful warning about the

Ides of October, and then disappeared. Which is what we knew before we interviewed the first person.

When the last person had been interviewed, Quintilian rose from his seat and began pacing back and forth across the room, his head down, looking at the floor in front of him. I scurried over to the side of the room and sat on the floor, my back against the wall, to keep out of his way. My mentor thinks best in motion, and I try to do nothing to disturb his thinking.

He stayed in motion for some time, gesticulating in strange and wonderful ways as he paced, grabbing thoughts and ideas from the air and assembling them into various patterns, until he found one that made sense out of the facts of the case. He had explained this to me many times, and I had watched him perform this magic in many different cases, usually shortly before the start of a trial. I say 'magic' because, when I try a similar process, all I grab is thin air, and all I get is a headache.

Finally he stopped pacing and sat

down. 'If something is impossible,' he said, 'why then, it is impossible. Discard it, and you are left with the truth.'

'What does that mean?' I asked.

He turned, seeming a bit surprised to see me squatting there against the wall. 'It means I see a way to catch a ghost.'

I shuddered. And, mind you, I'm not at all sure I believe in ghosts. But after the stories we had just heard . . . 'Is that wise?' I asked.

'Not only wise, but necessary,' he told me. 'It will require a long strand of wool, and, just in case, a man with an axe.'

'Pardon me?' I said.

'That centurion — Sabatinus — should be waiting somewhere outside the door. Fetch him for me.'

I went into the corridor and beckoned to the centurion, who was sitting on a chair he had acquired from somewhere, talking with two of his troopers. Sabatinus fairly trotted into the room. 'It's approaching dinner time,' he said. 'I would like to let my men go for their meal, if you can spare them for an hour or so.'

Quintilian pushed himself to his feet.

'Let us wind up this business,' he said, 'and then, no doubt, your men will be able to feast.'

'Ah!' Centurion Sabatinus said. 'Then, honorable Quintilian, you have been able to make some sense of the stories you have been listening to?'

'Send one of your men for an axe,' Quintilian told him, 'and have him meet us at the anteroom where that poor lad was found dead.'

Sabatinus sent one of his men off to find an axe, and he led the rest of us back to the door to the anteroom. Which was a good thing as, with all the twists and turns we took in this gigantic maze of a palace, I doubt whether we could have found it on our own.

'You wait out here,' Quintilian told us. 'I don't want you disturbing the air in the room.' And with the final comment, 'I could be wrong, but I think not,' he went inside the little room by himself.

We waited. We could hear pounding, tapping and thumping from inside for a while, and then my master stuck his head out the door. 'I need more light,' he said.

'Bring me some lamps.'

Sabatinus's men scattered about and found four lamps, returning with them about the same time as the trooper who had gone for the axe rejoined our little band. Quintilian took the lamps inside the room and closed the door. We waited some more. This time there was nothing but silence from inside the room.

Quintilian opened the door. 'Come in,' he said. 'We won't need the axe. Well, perhaps we will need the axe; bring it along.'

We followed him back into the room. 'Well, I'll be,' Centurion Sabatinus said.

At first I didn't see anything different, except for the circle of oil lamps burning on the floor, casting their varied shadows on the walls. And then I saw that what I had taken to be a shadow was actually an opening in the side wall. Starting at the floor, it was about two feet square, and seemed to lead into some sort of tunnel. The part of the wall that had concealed the tunnel had opened inward, and was now flat against the tunnel's side.

'Did you know there were secret

passages within the palace?' my master asked Sabatinus.

'There was a secret exit,' the centurion told him. 'It was the way that Nero escaped the mob that was hunting him, after hiding for a day. We have closed it up. How did you find this one?'

'Logic said there had to be an entrance to this room aside from the two doors. Even a ghost couldn't take a body through solid walls.'

'But a man could have passed the guards without attracting much attention,' Sabatinus said. 'Besides, in the middle of the night, there was a good chance the guards would be asleep — or at least dozing.'

'Yes, and a man might chance it. But I doubt whether a man carrying a body would feel the same. So the most logical answer was that there's a hidden entrance to this room. At first I tapped all the walls, but I couldn't detect any difference in sound. So then I pulled a strand of wool from the hem of my toga and lighted the end from one of the lamps. It burned with a thin wisp of black smoke. I slowly moved it about the room, near the walls, until I saw the smoke deflected by a slight draft. After some experimentation I found the panel unlocked by pushing in on a leaf in the wall painting, and then I could slide it open. So I didn't have to call on the axeman.'

Centurion Sabatinus nodded. 'Very logical,' he said.

'Let's see where this doorway leads,' Quintilian said.

'Wait,' said Sabatinus. 'I'll go first — that's my job.' Pulling his gladius from its scabbard, he held the short sword in front of him in his right hand and an oil lamp in his left, and crawled head-first into the tunnel. Quintilian followed, and then the three troopers, each with one of the oil lamps, and the last carrying the great double-bladed axe that he had brought. I followed in the rear, and glad of it. I am not made for fighting. And yet nothing could have stopped me from following along to see the end to this ghostly mystery.

After a short distance the tunnel turned to the left, and then rose steeply some six or eight feet and continued on. A little ways further — it's hard to judge distance when you're crawling — the ceiling rose and it was possible to walk upright. There was a steady breeze blowing through the tunnel; I could feel it on my face, and it made the flame in my lamp flicker.

The tunnel went down again, and then turned to the left, and we could see light ahead of us. After a few moments we came to a room, octagonal in shape, perhaps twelve or fourteen feet across, lighted by a sort of covered skylight, so that light came in from the sides but not from directly overhead. There was a table in the room with a pitcher of water and a mug, and there, on a chair by the table, sat Julius Caesar. His toga was soiled, and his fringe of hair was disheveled, but the resemblance was unmistakable. Several laurel wreaths hung from pegs on the wall.

'Don't kill me,' Caesar screeched, throwing himself under the table and cowering as we entered the room. 'Please don't kill me! It wasn't my fault. It wasn't my idea. Don't kill me!'

* * *

A quarter hour later we all stood before Vespasian and his son in the audience hall that the emperor — excuse me, the general — used for state business. 'Secret passages,' Vespasian said, 'running all through the palace. Who could have guessed?'

'Apparently Nero had them constructed as the palace was being built,' Quintilian told him. 'He used workers from the far provinces and then sent them home again, so the work would stay secret. That's according to our ghost, here.' He indicated the soiled Caesar, who was doing his best to stand straight and unafraid, despite the leather restraints with which he had been bound, still not convinced that he was not about to be beheaded.

Vespasian nodded. 'I suppose, knowing Nero, I should have thought of something like that,' he said.

'If you want to put stock in the sayings of the Sybil,' Quintilian said, 'you could take her first two lines:

'The past returns through the wiles of men
It is not hard to die

'as referring to the hidden passages. 'It is not hard to die,' should remind us of the day Nero spent hiding in this palace, and we should have asked ourselves just where it was that he hid.'

Vespasian nodded thoughtfully, and then turned his attention to the ghost. 'I await your story impatiently,' he said.

Caesar fell to his knees. 'My name, so it please your honor, is Lysidamus. I am from the island of Crete. I was brought here as a child and sold to a company of touring actors. It was never clear which of them actually owned me, and I suppose it didn't matter. I was eventually given small parts to play, usually girls or women. When my voice changed, I played the insolent slave, or on occasion the young lover — '

'Let's get to the part where you're hiding in secret passages in this palace,' Domitian interrupted.

'Yes, your honor. Of course, your honor. The emperor Nero saw me in a production of Plautus's *The Boy From Carthage* — I played the boy — and immediately purchased me and made me a freedman. I joined the imperial troupe of actors, and became Nero's voice coach. For when he played parts in Greek. He spoke Greek with a terrible Latin accent. I became adept at not quite telling him that.'

'Get to the secret passages,' Domitian said.

'Yes, your honor. The hidden corridors were used by Nero to spy on his enemies and, I suppose, his friends. There are tubes in the walls that can be uncapped and, if you put your ear to them, you can hear what is being said in the room outside. On that horrible day when the people turned against him, he hid at first in the secret rooms. I went with him, but when early the next day he fled the palace, I remained behind. I have been living in these secret places ever since, coming out only for food and to, ah, borrow clean garments.'

'Three, almost four, years?' Vespasian asked, incredulously.

'I believe so. One loses track of time in, ah, my situation.'

'Why did you stay?'

'At first through fear, I thought the subsequent emperors would just as soon eliminate all memories of Nero, and I was one of those memories. And then because I really had no place else to go.'

'You've been listening to what goes on here for all that time?' Domitian demanded.

'Oh, no!' Lysidamus said, sounding shocked. 'I never took the caps from the listening tubes. That wouldn't be right.'

'And just when did you become a ghost?' Vespasian asked.

'It must be over a year ago now. I was, let's see, in the pastry kitchen, I believe. Someone walked in on me while I was gathering a few pastries to take back to my lair. I raised my arms in fright, and much to my surprise, he was more frightened than I. He raced from the room screaming that he'd seen a ghost — Great Caesar's ghost, to be precise. And, of course, when the others came in to see, I was back in the wall.'

'Great Caesar's ghost?' Quintilian asked.

'Even that first time?'

'That's what the man said — yelled. I did not realize how much I had come to resemble the great Gaius Julius with the passage of time. I still thought of myself as the young lover. But I decided to take advantage of this chance resemblance and never leave my hidy-hole without wearing an imperial toga and a laurel wreath, and dusting my face with a little flour.'

Domitian glared at the sad little man. 'Sneaking into the imperial palace,' he said. 'That's a serious offense.'

'I don't know if we can get him for that,' Vespasian said, smiling. 'After all, he was here before we were.'

'Yes? Well, what about that 'Ides of October' nonsense?'

'I don't think he's responsible for that,' Quintilian said. 'Are you?' he asked Lysidamus.

'Well, I — '

'I mean you did it, of course, but you're not responsible for it.'

'Yes,' Domitian said, 'but murdering that lad . . . '

Quintilian turned back to Domitian.

'Oh, that he didn't do.'

'Then what did he do?'

'He was discovered,' Quintilian said. 'Weren't you?' He leaned over Lysidamus. 'Weren't you?'

'Yes, yes.'

'By whom?' asked Vespasian.

'I don't know his name. He caught me about a month ago, while I was making my nightly foray for a loaf of bread, and ever since I've been living in fear. He told me that, were he to turn me in, I would be instantly executed. But he said he had use for me. He explored the secret ways and found places for me to appear. He told me what to say. Last night, when a young lad almost caught me he — he took away the lad's little knife, and jabbed at him with long stiletto that he kept concealed in his toga. I think he killed him.'

'You don't know?'

'He told me to go back to my room. I went.'

'He did kill the lad,' Quintilian told Lysidamus.

The actor burst out sobbing and fell to

the floor. 'What a pity, what a pity,' he cried. 'And he was such a handsome lad!'

'Who did this?' Vespasian asked.

'I swear, I don't know his name,' Lysidamus sobbed. 'He wears a senatorial toga.'

'His name is Marius Trabitus,' Quintilian told Vespasian. 'He is a senator.'

'Trabitus?' Vespasian repeated. 'Why, I know him. He told me he actually saw the ghost, I remember. He has been spending a lot of time in the palace. He knows of my intention to move, and has an interest in taking the building over to turn it into an I-don't-know-what. Some sort of forum, or such. Or so he told me.'

'I think you'll find he's associated with one of the groups you mentioned that has its own ideas about who should be emperor,' Quintilian said. 'Perhaps he thought that if he made enough noise about the 'Ides of October,' some superstitious guardsman or courtier would think the gods were giving him instructions.'

'And why do you name this Trabitus as the instigator?'

'And as the murderer of young Septius.

He would have been better served by keeping the youth's body hidden. Ghostly appearances are one thing, who knows about ghosts? But a corpse lying in a room has to have arrived there somehow. I knew it was he when he told me of seeing bloody wounds on the ghost of Caesar; an obvious, ah, exaggeration. Why would he make such things up were he not involved? And then he told me that little knives are no defense against ghosts. But nobody knew that lad had a knife, since the sheath was concealed under his body until I turned him over. Bring Trabitus here and let our actor friend identify him.'

'I shall,' Vespasian said, and gave the order.

*   *   *

Trabitus was not found in the palace and, by the time a squad of the Praetorian Guard reached his villa, he had committed suicide by slitting his wrists in the bath. When Lysidamus was taken to look at the body, he identified Trabitus as the man who had caught him, and who murdered Septius.

It was about a month later that Vespasian created the Imperial Office of Teaching Rhetoric to the Young, and appointed my master Quintilian to be its head.

> *The highly regarded ignorant one will*
>   *cleave the knot*
> *And Caesar shall create a school in*
>   *his answer*

How does the Sybil know these things?

3

Four Hundred Slaves

It was in the sixth year of the reign of the Emperor Vespasian that this story of the exploits of my master, the great orator and logician Marcus Fabius Quintilianus, begins. I use the word 'master' in the sense of 'teacher' or 'fount of all wisdom,' rather than in the slaveholding sense, since I, Plautus Maximilianus Aureus, the great Quintilian's pupil and scribe, am a freeborn citizen of Rome. I point this out because the distinction is an important one and, in the story I am about to relate, it is a matter of life or death.

A flock of shrikes settled in the olive grove outside our villa in the afternoon of the third day of the Nones of April, and two of the shrill, nasty little birds proceeded to have a screaming argument, while the others called their encouragement from the surrounding trees. Susannah, a young recently-acquired slave from the East, came out and stood beside me in the atrium at dusk, clutching her arms about her under her breasts, which were just large enough to provide an interesting contour beneath her white robe, and we listened to the birds fussing and screeching.

I affected no notice of her contours. Since Quintilian was showing an interest in his new possession, an interest that seemed to be welcomed gratefully, perhaps even eagerly, it would be pointless and unwise. Besides there was Adella, one of the household maids, who had indicated with many a giggle that she would not strongly resist my advances.

Susannah shivered as the birds set off a new round of raucous dissent. 'It is an ill portent,' she said earnestly.

'The shrieking of these miserable birds signifies something?' I asked.

'Death,' she said with a shudder.

Quintilian came out and stood behind us. 'Whose death?' he asked smiling down at her. 'And how will he die? Pecked to death, perhaps?'

She raised her little fists and beat them in frustration against Quintilian's chest. A capital crime, striking her master; but he did not seem to regard it so. 'You don't take me seriously,' she said. 'But I know what I know.'

Quintilian drew more tightly around him the wool mantle he had thrown on. 'I'll have Capulus throw some stones at the flock,' he said. 'Get them to move on.'

'It won't help,' the girl said solemnly. 'They have settled at dusk and are screaming their screams, and someone will die.' Somehow her lilting Aramaic — I think it was Aramaic — accent gave the pronouncement more weight, and I felt an involuntary shiver run down my spine.

Quintilian sighed. 'An easy prediction to make,' he said. '"Someone will die." Undoubtedly someone will die. Disease, accident, treachery, war; it's amazing that any of us manage to survive.'

'Someone will die whose death has meaning to you,' she insisted. 'Perhaps more than one.'

He looked from one to the other of us. I think he could see that, try as I might to remain unmoved, her words were troubling me. A portent is, after all, a portent. And her name might not be Cassandra, but who knew what prophetic powers were granted to the Susannahs of this world?

'I am approaching my forty-fifth birthday,' my master said, 'and many whom I care about and a few whom I despise have left this world already. I have no doubt that more will follow.'

'Throwing stones at the flock will not help,' Susannah said.

Quintilian took a deep breath. 'What would help?' he asked.

'I know of nothing,' Susannah said, shaking her head sadly.

'Well then, a few stones might at least get us a quiet night's sleep,' Quintilian said. 'And what the gods choose to do they will do, regardless. I will give instructions. Join me in the bedchamber shortly.'

Susannah touched her finger to her forehead in what I have learned is an Oriental gesture of obedience.

Quintilian nodded and left us.

Before I went to bed that night I took a jug of vinegar and some sprigs of dried rosemary from the pantry and poured a line of vinegar across all the entrances to the villa, pouring only with my left hand, keeping the rosemary in my right hand over my head, and reciting as I went the witching poem I remembered from my childhood: 'Nuncus rebus mangus poppis; Halifratus satum flebis.' I placed a twig of rosemary at each end of each vinegary line. What language the witching poem might be, or indeed if the words had meaning in any language, I know not. But the combination of vinegar and verse was said to ward off danger and misfortune, and the rosemary kept away evil. I didn't know whether it would work against shrikes or not, but as my old nurse used to say, 'It couldn't hurt.'

Peris, the door slave, gave me unasked-for advice on tending to an addled pate. He had always thought I was slightly crazy, and watching me go from portal to portal, limping (from a childhood injury), mumbling and pouring, did little to disabuse him of this notion.

Did it work? I can't say. Perhaps things would have been even worse had I not gone through that little ceremony, perhaps it was all just vinegar and rosemary and mumbled nonsense; only the gods know for sure. What I do know is that it was the next day that we learned of the first death.

Quintilian was to teach his class in advanced rhetoric that day. The students arrived in a batch in the forenoon; twelve of them, sons of some of Rome's most important and distinguished men, all in early manhood. They gathered in a corner of the atrium where benches had been placed in a semicircle around a point from which the speaker of the moment could declaim.

Since the emperor Vespasian had created the Chair of Literature and Rhetoric for my master, and given him the task of devising the ideal curriculum for the youth of Rome, the fees he commanded for teaching were approaching the Olympian. And this in addition to the generous stipend from the imperial purse that went with his position. On the other hand, at least two of his students paid no fees, and one I knew, whose father's estates had been confiscated by Nero, owed sandals, tunic and toga to my master.

The subject on which the students were to discourse convincingly was an old standard: if Sister Verga, one of the Vestal priestesses, was thrown off a cliff for having violated her oath and somehow survived; should the punishment be deemed to have been carried out, or should she be thrown off the cliff again?

But another death occupied them this day. The talk in the forum was of the murder of Cassius Caprius Strabo, who had been found dead of a knife thrust in his own study. A onetime magistrate and Procurator of Bithynia before he retired to his villa on the northern outskirts of Rome, the honorable Strabo was a direct descendant of the great Pompey, and was — or I should say had been — highly regarded for his judgment and his sense of morality. Indeed, he was one of the *amici*, the 'special friends' from whom the Emperor Vespasian sought advice. And he had been a good friend of Quintilian. Indeed it had only been a week or so before that my master had attended a dinner party in Strabo's honor.

Quintilian insisted that the class go on, even though several of the students, especially those who were to speak that day, expressed their willingness to delay the class until a better time.

Thestis, Quintilian's major domo, came out to the atrium and waited patiently while young Crassus Hypotus, with many a 'Hear me, O Rome,' forcefully explained that, having once been thrown off the cliff, Sister Verga had been placed in the hands of the gods, and all mortal punishments had been satisfied. Throwing her off the cliff again would be an affront to the gods' judgment. I was convinced. But then I always find myself convinced by the last speaker, whichever side he was on, in any argument. Such is the power of rhetoric.

When Crassus finally bowed to the student playing presiding judge and sat down, Thestis went over and whispered in Quintilian's ear. Quintilian rose and said, 'You've all been most sincere and convincing. Now each of you who spoke today prepare to speak for the other side. Lose none of your sincerity while advocating the opposite view; that is the mark of the true master of rhetoric. I'll hear you when I return.' He beckoned to me and crossed the atrium. I trotted, or perhaps limped, after him.

Thestis pointed us toward the front of the villa. 'I placed him in the fore-yard,' he said. 'He asked for a cup of watered wine, which I had sent to him. Although, by the way he looks, he could use more of the wine and less of the water.'

Quintilian turned to me. 'Come, Scribbler. You have your writing tablets and stylus? Good. Sit in a corner and take discreet notes.'

'Scribbler' is my less than elegant nick-name. But I don't mind. Many, including some famous and well-respected men, have been called worse. 'Yes, sir,' I said. 'Don't I always?'

'Sometimes you are more discreet than others,' he replied. 'Let this be one of those times.'

Waiting for us on a bench in the sunny fore-yard was a young man in a spotless white toga. He had brown eyes, an artfully bent nose, and a mass of unruly brown hair. An expression that hinted of panic was frozen on his otherwise unlined patrician face. He jumped to his feet at our approach. 'Master Quintilian,' he said. 'Thank you for seeing me.'

'How could I not?' said Quintilian. 'One of my best pupils; the son of one of my closest friends.' He sat beside the youth on the bench. 'I heard about your father, and I am very sorry. All of Rome grieves.'

So this was Marius Strabo, son of the murdered Cassius Strabo. I knew that he had been a pupil of Quintilian, but I had never met him before. I squatted on the ground by the bench and took a wax tablet and stylus from my pouch. My main task is recording what of any import is said to and by Quintilian. Periodically I transcribe those words that might be wanted again onto fine Egyptian papyrus, which is sorted by subject and date. Quintilian has for years been working on several books: a record of his cases and orations, a book of instruction for those who would teach the young, a textbook on rhetoric, a collection of his poetry, and a history of Roman law. The collected sheets of papyrus grow, and occasionally my master leafs through one or another of them and says something like, 'What was that clever thing I said about a student being like a butterfly?' or, 'Where is a copy of the reply I wrote to Martial's nasty little quatrain a couple of years back?' If I'm lucky I remember, and can find it. If not I tell him and he says, 'No matter, no matter, you can't be expected to remember everything.' Which hurts like the sting of a lash, for what good am I, poor cripple that I am, if I cannot even remember the location of everything in the small universe that is Quintilian's writings?

'It is that which I have come to see you about,' Marius said. 'What have you heard of my father's murder?'

'Only what is common knowledge in the Forum,' Quintilian told him. 'And what is common knowledge is almost always deficient in detail and inaccurate in fact. Why don't you tell me what you would have me know.'

Marius nodded and took several breaths before commencing. 'My father was killed in his study, which is a small separate house resting against the back wall of the villa. There are three rooms; an office, a library and, past those, a small chamber with a couch on which father used to rest during the day. He was in the first room, his office, at his desk, apparently working on his numbering system when he was stabbed in the side by a long, thin blade.'

'Numbering system?' I asked.

Marius looked at me as though seeing me for the first time. 'Yes,' he said. 'My father worked with figures his whole life; collecting the taxes in Bithynia, supplying and paying the legions under his command, and of late trying to devise a more rational and just tax collection system for the empire, at the emperor's request. And he still works with the Quartermaster Corps, seeing that equipment and supplies destined for his old legions are of good quality and price. He believed that the — I think it was — Phoenician numbers are easier to use than our own. You know: adding, multiplying; that sort of thing. He was trying to adapt Phoenician numbers to Roman needs.' Marius shrugged and his eyes fell. 'I suppose the idea died with Father. I confess to having scant interest in the subject, and none of those working with or under him have any interest in it at all, as far as I can tell.'

'The abacus works well enough for most calculations,' Quintilian commented.

'It was while discussing the use of the abacus with Pliny that Father got the idea for his system,' Marius told him. 'The abacus is fine as long as you don't make a mistake but, as Pliny pointed out, an error, even a large error, can go unnoticed, due to our cumbersome reckoning system. Or so said my father.'

'Ah!' said Quintilian, and waited while the young man stared off into space and allowed some strong emotion to wash over him.

Marius suddenly gripped Quintilian's arm. 'You have to help me, sir,' he said. 'I don't know what to do!'

Quintilian gently disengaged the lad's hand from his arm. 'What is it that you want done?' he asked mildly.

Marius drained his glass of watered wine. Thestis, who stood silently in a corner by a large potted plant, immediately filled it again from a pitcher he was holding.

'A slave has been accused of the killing,' Marius said. 'His name is Prusias. I've known him since I was a small child.' He shook his head. 'I cannot believe that he did this, yet the evidence against him is overwhelming.'

'Do you want me to prosecute him or defend him?' Quintilian asked.

Marius stared at him mutely for a minute, and then shook his head. 'Would it were that simple,' he said. 'I am not clear as to what I want you to do — or what you can do.'

'Tell me what you know,' Quintilian said. 'How did it happen?'

'It was yesterday,' Marius said, 'shortly after the noon meal. I was not there at the time.'

'Where were you?' Quintilian interrupted.

Marius flushed. 'I was at a house on the

121

Via Claudia,' he said. 'A gambling house. While my father was being murdered, I was throwing dice. I won three denarii, and came home to find my father dead. The gods laugh.'

'So you have no direct knowledge of what happened?'

'I didn't see the murder, if that's what you mean,' said Marius. 'I arrived home just as my father's body was discovered.'

'Tell me about it.'

Marius put a finger to his nose and stared at the ceiling briefly. People often do that — the staring, not the nose — when they're arranging their thoughts. I wonder why. 'The sun was low in the sky when I returned home,' Marius said. 'I was told Father was working in his study. Just as I reached the courtyard everyone began running about and screaming and moaning that the procurator was dead. It took me a moment to realize that it was my father they were talking about.'

'Everybody?'

'Everybody in the courtyard at the time. Someone had knocked on the door to the study and got no response, so he went to the window and peered in. He saw my father lying dead across his desk. And the only person who'd been in the room all afternoon was Prusias, who brought my father a cup of watered lemon juice and some olives and flat bread. Father doesn't — didn't — like to be disturbed while at work.'

'And this was when Prusias shoved a knife in his side?'

'So they say. There is no other answer.'

'What knife? From where?'

'It is a thin blade of Persian design. No one knows where it came from. No one in the household has ever been seen to have one like it in his or her possession.'

'Did your father try to fight off his attacker?'

'Fight off?' Marius thought about it. 'No. He was seated at his desk, his head fallen among his papyri. He looked, except for the knife sticking out of his side, as though he had fallen asleep.'

'Interesting,' Quintilian said. 'What motive did Prusias have?'

'Motive? None that I know of.'

'What does he say happened?'

Marius let out a sudden burst of laughter that startled us. I think it startled him. 'Prusias says nothing,' he explained. 'He cannot speak. His tongue was cut out and his vocal cords severed when he was much younger.' He looked from one to the other of us and saw that we were staring at him.

'I cannot believe my old friend Strabo would do such a thing,' Quintilian said.

'I'm sorry,' said Marius. 'I have lived with Prusias for so long that I forgot how that would sound. The, ah, mutilation had been done to him before my father acquired him from a slave dealer in Nicomedia; we never found out why.'

'So Prusias has been with your family for a long time?'

'At least twenty-five years.'

'And he suddenly decided to kill his master? For no reason that you know of?'

'So it would seem.'

Quintilian signaled to Thestis to bring him a cup of watered wine and looked thoughtfully at a pot of African lilies while the wine was poured. 'Let us go over this and see if we can create a rational picture,' he said. 'Prusias, who cannot speak — ' he interrupted himself to ask, 'Can he understand?'

'Simple commands,' Marius said. 'Perhaps more.'

'Ah!' Quintilian said. 'So this simple mute slave, after serving your family faithfully — I assume — for a quarter of a century, suddenly decided to kill his master. Strabo offered no resistance, indeed seemed not to notice when his trusted slave produced a long, thin knife along with the drink — a knife which appeared from nowhere, and which the slave was not seen to be carrying when he delivered the watered lemon juice . . . '

'How do you know that?'

'Pah!' Quintilian said. 'You would have mentioned it if anyone had seen him with a knife. And he leaves the knife behind. In the wound, presumably?'

'Yes.'

'And just goes calmly about his work?'

'Yes,' Marius said. 'And no one was seen to enter the study after Prusias left. And Father *is* dead.'

'True,' Quintilian agreed. 'And there were people in the courtyard the whole time?'

'The whole time.'

'Who?'

'My aunt Prunella and her daughter, my cousin Lucasta. My aunt is tutoring Lucasta in Greek.'

'Good!' Quintilian declared. 'Women should be educated. We need more educated women to make up for the great excess of foolish men.' He gave me a sideways glance to be sure I had gotten that down. It would probably appear in one of his texts, if he ever got around to writing them.

'And a gardener,' Marius continued, 'and a couple of men fixing the drains.'

'Which of them found him?' Quintilian asked.

'Actually it was a business acquaintance of my father's. A senator named Gaius Veccus.'

'Business?'

'Yes,' Marius said. 'I know senators don't usually sully their togas with business, but if two or three of your clients start a factory with money you've loaned them and then insist on making you a partner, well, what are you to do?'

'What indeed?' Quintilian agreed.

'Veccus has a couple of factories full of slaves making shields, leather leggings, helmets; that sort of thing. All the trappings of war,' Marius explained. 'And Father was acquiring military supplies for the VII and IX Legions in Western Gaul.'

Quintilian thought it over. 'It's interesting,' he said. 'If the mute slave killed your father, why did he, and why is it that nobody heard? And where did he get the knife? If, on the other hand, Prusias didn't kill Strabo, then who did, and how did he manage it?'

'That's the problem,' Marius agreed.

'I don't know whether I'd rather prosecute or defend,' Quintilian said. 'Which reminds me, which is it that you want me to do?'

'Neither,' said Marius. 'My problem is other than that.'

Quintilian leaned forward. 'Yes?'

I don't know what my master expected to hear, but I'm sure it wasn't what he heard.

127

'If Prusias is convicted of killing my father,' Marius said, 'then all the slaves owned by my father are to be put to death. All four hundred. I cannot allow that to happen. I cannot.'

Quintilian looked shocked; something I had seldom seen. 'Four hundred?' he asked.

Marius nodded. 'Just about. Some are at farms down south, some at warehouses in Ostia or in the city. The total is about four hundred. And they are all to be put to death. And whoever the magistrates decide are the ringleaders are to be tortured first.'

'Come now,' Quintilian said. 'That used to be the custom — putting to death all the slaves in a household if one should slay his master. But it hasn't been followed for a hundred years. Well, eighty, at least.'

'It's being insisted on by the Senate,' Marius said. 'Because of my father's status and position. They say an example must be made.'

'And what does Vespasian say about this?'

'So far the emperor has not spoken.' Marius shook his head as though to clear it of unwelcome thoughts. 'This cannot happen,' he continued. 'You must find a way to stop it.'

Quintilian shaded his eyes from the bright sun to peer at the young man. 'So,' he said. 'With your father dead, you will now inherit the slaves. You're protecting a financial interest.'

'No, no,' Marius protested. 'Not at all. The slaves — all of them — were to be manumitted upon the death of my father. It's in his will. They were even to be given small businesses, or enough money to start their own.'

'I see,' Quintilian said. 'You want me to find a way to prevent the executions of the slaves owned by your father, all of which were to be freed upon his death.'

'Yes,' Marius said eagerly. 'Can you?'

'I don't know,' Quintilian said, shaking his head. 'It seems that each of them had a good reason to wish for the death of your father.'

'Not by murder,' Marius said. 'If a conspiracy could be shown, they'd be put to death anyway.'

'That's so,' Quintilian agreed. 'And there's no hint of such a thing?'

'I'd say it was impossible.'

'What of Prusias?'

Marius shook his head. 'If he did it, he should pay. Although, as I said, I cannot believe that he did. But there is no reason why the other slaves, completely blameless I am sure, should be punished. Can you see a way to save them?'

'It would have to be argued before the Senate,' Quintilian said thoughtfully. 'I would be speaking for the murdered man's son, and that would carry some weight. Although I think it would actually help if they weren't being manumitted. A financial interest speaks louder than a desire for mercy, people being what they are.'

'I will reward you with a large honorarium if you make the attempt,' Marius said. 'And even more — much more — should you be successful.'

Orators who try cases in the criminal courts or plead before the Senate are supposed to be doing it for the love of the law, of truth and justice, and of the people of Rome; and, of course, a belief in their cause. They are not, by tradition, to require a fee. But if their client should happen to present them with a gift at the end of the case, as a token of his esteem and gratitude, it would be ungrateful to turn it down.

'Very well,' Quintilian said, draining his cup of wine and setting it down. 'You have presented me with an interesting challenge, and I'll see what I can do. On the one hand it is obviously an injustice that three hundred and ninety-nine innocent slaves should be punished for the actions of one — if, indeed, he is guilty. On the other, slave rebellions are horrible things, which lead to excesses of cruelty and death on both sides. Anything that could tend to suppress or prevent one, even if cruel in itself, could be said to prevent a greater cruelty — by those,' Quintilian continued, seeing the horrified look on Marius's face, 'who would say such things.'

'My father's slaves contemplated no rebellion,' Marius said. 'They were promised their freedom; why should they take such a foolhardy risk?'

'Why indeed,' Quintilian said, leaning back. 'Tell me what you are not telling me.'

'What? Tell you what?'

'There is something more, something you're avoiding mentioning,' Quintilian said. 'I can sense it.'

Marius blushed. 'If so,' he said, 'it is nothing that can affect what I have asked you to do — I swear it!'

Quintilian rose to his feet. 'I'll see what can be done,' he said. 'I must visit the scene and speak to those who were there. Also to your household slaves.'

'Of course,' said Marius. 'I must return to the villa to do — ' He paused and gathered himself. 'To do what remains to be done. Arrange with the undertaker for the funeral procession for my father; the band, the paid mourners — although there will be many who mourn without pay — and prepare the family tomb out along the *Via Appia*. I am told that the emperor will be at the villa sometime during the week of mourning, so preparations for his visit must be made. You may come by at your will. I must see about getting servants to run the household for the near future. The household slaves have been taken to the city slave pens until their disposition is decided.' He hit his right fist into his left palm several times in a distracted, and probably painful, way. 'I must also do what I can for them — provide food, clothing and bedding. That which is provided by the aedile in charge of the slave pens is not fit for — for — for slaves.'

Marius left, his steps slow and positive; the mind willing the body to do what it would not.

Quintilian turned to look down at me. 'Well?' he asked.

I gathered my tools and put them back in their small sack. 'Well, what, master?' I asked.

'Well, what do you think we should do first?' he asked. This is his way of instructing me.

'I'm sorry, master, I have no idea,' I told him. This is my way of learning.

'Should we go first to the slave pens, or

to the Strabo villa?' he amplified.

I thought for a second. 'The villa,' I said.

'Why?'

'Because I have no desire to go to the slave pens. They are smelly, foul, horrible, degrading, depressing — '

He nodded. 'You're right, they are all of that. Despite that, I think we'd best visit the slave pens first, and the villa after.'

Why, then, in the name of the Seven Fates did you ask me? I thought. What I said was, 'As you say, Master Quintilian.'

'Refresh yourself with some bread and cheese, and perhaps a fig; we'll leave shortly.'

Quintilian can't help it, he tells everyone what to do. 'Bread, cheese and a fig' indeed! As though I couldn't choose my own lunch.

I had bread and cheese and a handful of black olives, and waited for him by the door. He appeared shortly wearing sturdier sandals and a broad farmer's hat. Susannah came running up behind him carrying a dark brown woolen cloak. 'Take this,' she urged, handing it to him.

'You'll be out late, and it gets quite chilly these evenings.' She looked at me. 'You, too,' she said. 'Take a cloak.'

Quintilian grunted his thanks and strode out the door. I grabbed an old cloak from a peg by the door and hurried out after him, as he headed off down the street. Two bodyguards fell into step behind us. It isn't particularly dangerous to walk around Rome in the daylight, but nobody who is anybody travels anywhere without bodyguards. Praetors go everywhere accompanied by six lictors — official bodyguards paid by the state — consuls have twelve.

Quintilian walked everywhere. I have seldom seen him use a sedan chair or a litter. And his normal pace would be considered a forced march by a legionary. Even our tall, blond Gaulish bodyguards had to lengthen their strides to keep up, and were breathing deeply after the first half hour. I limped along the best I could without complaining; I had not sufficient breath to utter a complaint.

The slave pens are, as you might suspect, not in one of the better sections of Rome. The large, squat enclosure is way out on the Via Lubicana, past blocks of tenements that lean and spew garbage and occasionally collapse, burying their tenants. The pens are enclosed by a high brick wall. Their inner walls are brick, wood, or iron bars, depending. The roof, over that part that has a roof, is wood. The smell is indescribable. The sounds that come from it combine all the musical elements of an abattoir and an iron forge.

Quintilian strode up to the gate, where he was stopped by two large guards, ex-gladiators, by the look of them, who demanded to know just who he thought he was, marching up to the gate like that. Our own escorts looked amused, but they didn't look as though they relished the idea of getting in a dispute with the hulking guards.

'I'd like to see the aedile in charge of the pens,' Quintilian said.

'Oh, really?' said one of the guards. 'And what makes you think His Excellency Lepidus would spend his time down here at the pens when he has better things to do?'

'Better places to be,' added the other guard.

'I see,' Quintilian said. 'Then who is in charge here?'

'As it happens,' said the first guard, 'His Excellency Lepidus is here today.'

'Pure chance,' said the other. 'Sometimes weeks go by and we don't see him.'

Quintilian gathered his cloak around him. 'Would you tell His Excellency Lepidus that Marcus Fabius Quintilianus would speak with him, on the emperor's business.'

'On the emperor's business?' guard one repeated.

'Why didn't you say so?' asked guard two. 'You only have two bodyguards, how were we to know?'

'I'll go myself,' declared guard one, and disappeared into the interior of the compound.

'Don't stand outside,' guard two exclaimed, opening the door wide, 'come and wait inside.'

We entered into a large open area surrounded by brick walls and heavy barred doors. From all around us came the sounds of moaning, screeching, crying, screaming, bellowing, and what might have been chanting or singing. Strangely, none of the words were intelligible. Some distance across the large yard six or seven naked men were chained to large posts set in the earth. They did not seem to be enjoying themselves. Two of them were either unconscious or dead. One of them was looking up so that the sunlight shone directly on his face, and he seemed to be talking energetically to someone whom none of the rest of us could see.

Quintilian seated himself on a rude wooden bench inside the yard. 'The emperor's business?' I murmured to him, sitting on the other end of the bench.

'The proper administration of justice *is* the emperor's business,' he told me, with a stern glance. But perhaps there was the slightest hint of a smile at the corners of his mouth.

A little, fussy, gray-haired man who wasn't quite bald and wasn't quite fat came out of one of the doors across the yard accompanied by a tall, thin man with a balding pate, hawk-like eyes close together above a beak of a nose, and a senatorial toga.

'Eh, what's this,' the fussy man asked, approaching us.

'Are you the aedile Lepidus?' Quintilian asked.

'That I am.'

'The four hundred slaves from the Strabo household,' Quintilian said. 'I would like to see them.'

The senator interjected his beak into the discussion. 'And what business,' he asked in a voice as dry as fallen leaves, 'would you have with a bunch of rebellious slaves?'

'I am here on the emperor's business,' my master said. 'My name is Marcus Fabius Quintilianus. What is your interest in this?'

'I am Senator Veccus,' the hawked-nosed man said. 'I have a personal interest in seeing that these' — he waved his hand dismissively at some invisible slaves — 'vermin should be punished for their perfidy. I had the misfortune to be the one to find Procurator Strabo's body.'

'Ah, yes,' said Quintilian. 'So I have

heard. It must have been quite a shock.'

'It was. I had been speaking with him only a short time before.' Veccus shook his head sadly. 'He was an honorable and upright man.'

'We don't have anything like four hundred of them slaves,' the aedile said. 'Sixty-seven is what we've got. The others are from the late Strabo's farms to the south. They haven't got here yet.'

'I see,' Quintilian said. 'Let me see the ones you've got.'

'No point to it,' Lepidus said. 'They're going to be crucified, the lot of them. You can't buy them; you can't even make an offer.'

'Nonetheless I'd like to see them. Particularly the one — Prusias.'

'The one who did it? Going to examine him, are you? For the emperor? You won't get anything out of him. We put him to the torture for two hours before we figured out that he couldn't talk. He ain't got no tongue. The torturer wanted to keep at it anyway, but the senator and I figured there wasn't no point to it, so I sent him back to the cage with the others.'

140

'Very sensible,' Quintilian agreed. 'And who gave you the authority to torture a prisoner awaiting trial?'

Lepidus looked offended. 'You don't think as how I'd do that without orders, do you?' he asked. 'Take a chance of ending up under the lash myself? No.' He pointed a thumb at the lanky senator. 'The orders came direct from the senator here himself.'

'Indeed?'

'On behalf of the Senate,' Veccus affirmed. 'I thought we could wring the truth out of him — why he did it, who else was involved, that sort of thing. I didn't know he was, ah . . . ' He made a pinching gesture with his fingers in the general direction of his mouth.

'I can imagine your surprise,' Quintilian said dryly. He indicated the posts on the other side of the yard. 'Is that where you torture prisoners?'

'Nah,' the aedile said. 'We have a small yard set aside for that. Those posts are where we chain slaves who are being left out to die.' He pursed his lips. 'It's a funny thing; we need special permission to torture a slave, but if one causes trouble, we can just leave them out to die, and that's just fine.'

'Funny, indeed,' Quintilian agreed.

Lepidus shook his head. 'What is Rome coming to?' he asked. 'Come this way.' He led the way across the courtyard to a pair of large, wooden doors, with Veccus stalking along behind. 'We got them penned up in here. Emptied one of the common pens out and reserved it just for them.'

'Men and women together?' I asked.

Lepidus looked at me and frowned. 'None of that!' he said. 'The pen is split in half: men on one side, women on the other. If we let them mix together, no telling what they'd do.'

I thought I could tell him what they'd do, but I kept my mouth closed.

Lepidus pulled open the right-side door and ushered us into an area with an earth floor strewn with straw, a wood ceiling, and iron bars for walls. The room was divided into four separate barred cages, built to hold human beings. About thirty men of all ages, some in tunics of varying degrees of cleanliness and repair, some clad only in loin cloths, were sitting or lying about in various positions of discomfort in one of the cages, and a like number of women were huddled together for mutual support in the next. The other two were, for the moment, empty.

'Look at that,' Senator Veccus said, nodding toward the women's cage. 'A dove among crows.' He crossed to the cage, leaned against the bars, and pointed a finger inside. 'You there!' he called into the cluster of women. 'What's your name?'

The women scattered like pigeons across the cage. Veccus's pointing finger followed one of them. 'Yes you. Come over here. Don't be shy.'

The girl slowly crossed the cage as though pushing her way through a vat full of honey toward Veccus's beckoning finger. She appeared to be about seventeen, with cropped blonde hair framing an oval face. Her body, its lines revealed as it moved under her stained robe, would provoke thoughts in Jove that would severely annoy Juno. And yet she seemed possessed of an ethereal innocence, and

143

sweetness of disposition. I knew all of this within the first few seconds of seeing her; how I cannot say, it is indeed one of the eternal mysteries.

'Your name,' repeated the senator. 'I asked you your name.'

'Edissa, master,' she replied unwillingly, stopping a few feet short of the bars.

'Edissa. Greek, is it?' he asked, smiling a meaningless smile and rubbing his thumbs together.

'I'm from Syracuse, master,' she said so softly I could barely make out the words.

'So,' Veccus said. 'I've never had one from Syracuse before.' He turned to Lepidus. 'I want to, ah, examine this one. Prepare a private room for us.'

Lepidus bowed and turned to leave. The girl looked as though the vat of honey she had waded through had just risen up and engulfed her. She fought to breathe.

'Wait!' commanded Quintilian.

Like the scene in Plautus's *Bacchides* where the goddess Venus stops the hero in mid-stride, Lepidus froze with one foot off the ground and one arm extended.

Veccus turned, an incredulous look on his face.

'None of these slaves will be removed, or separated from the others, or questioned any further without the express permission of the emperor Vespasian until this investigation is over,' Quintilian told them. He turned to Lepidus, who was just putting his foot down. 'I shall hold you personally responsible.'

Lepidus nodded twice and clasped his hands together.

'Well, I — ' Veccus paused for a deep breath. 'If this is all the respect you have for the Senate, well then I have nothing more to say!' He gathered his toga about him and stalked out of the building.

The girl folded to the ground and began to sob quietly.

Quintilian came up next to the bars of the cage holding the men. 'I am Marcus Fabius Quintilianus,' he told them, speaking softly but clearly. It is a trick of oratory to speak softly at certain times; your audience must listen closely, which forces them to pay attention. 'Marius Strabo has asked me to come speak to you and learn what there is to be learned. He wants to help you. The emperor is also interested in your case.' Quintilian added that for the benefit of Lepidus, who was listening carefully to what was being said. 'Are there any among you,' he continued, 'who know anything about the murder of your master, or know of any reason why anyone would want to kill him?'

There was a silence from within the cage, as all the men inside stared at my master suspiciously. Then came a horrible inarticulate moan, as if someone's very soul were being unbearably squeezed. The men moved aside, and we saw an old man huddled in the corner, crouched on his knees with his head half buried in the straw. His back and his arms were caked with dried blood, which glistened with a black sheen in the half-light of the pens.

'Open the door to this pen,' Quintilian snapped at the aedile, 'and go fetch some rags soaked in vinegar and some clean toweling.'

Lepidus's mouth dropped open. 'You want me to fetch?'

'Well then fetch someone to fetch,' Quintilian said. 'And quickly! Torturing a slave suspected of a crime is one thing; letting him die while the investigation is not yet completed is quite another.'

That was a sentiment that Lepidus could understand, as was shown by the speed with which he threw the bolt on the door to the pen, and left the area. Quintilian's actual belief, that torture was barbaric and pointless, that whipping or caning students actually harmed the learning process, that torturing slaves merely induced them to say whatever they thought you wanted them to say (unless, of course, they had no tongue), would have puzzled, if not shocked, Lepidus.

Quintilian entered the pen and knelt by the side of the bloody old man. 'Prusias, I presume,' he said.

The old man made a keening sound.

'Why don't you lie down,' Quintilian said, 'and we'll cleanse your wounds.'

'He can't lie down, master,' said a young boy, coming up beside Quintilian and standing straight and stiff as an olive tree, his hands at his sides. 'His back is awful ripped up from the whip, and a couple of his ribs are broken from the club, so he can't lie down, back or front.'

'Club?' asked Quintilian.

'Yes, master.'

Quintilian sighed a deep and heart-felt sigh. 'How unnecessary,' he said. 'How foolish.'

'Yes, master,' the boy agreed.

Prusias said something. At least I assumed he was saying something. It came out as a series of grunts, puffs, squeaks, and snorts. Quintilian looked around. 'Can any of you understand him?' he asked.

'He says he didn't do nothing and he don't know why this is happening to him,' called a woman from the adjoining pen. A number of the women had clustered about the bars facing the men's pen and were watching us with expressions ranging from mild interest to stark terror.

Quintilian turned to her. 'You understand him?' he asked. 'What's your name?'

'I'm Ambrollia,' she said. 'He works for me in the kitchen. I've been understanding him for fourteen years.'

'Well, Ambrollia, I'm going to ask him

some questions,' Quintilian said. 'You tell me what he says.'

She looked at him suspiciously, and then shrugged. 'It can't get us in any worse trouble,' she said. 'You go ahead.'

Quintilian began questioning Prusias, and Prusias grunted his replies. Ambrollia listened to the grunts and translated them for us. While this was going on a man built like two gladiators stuffed inside each other brought in a bucket of vinegar and some reasonably clean rags, and Quintilian put the boy to cleansing Prusias's wounds. If the vinegar stung, Prusias didn't seem to notice. I guess he was beyond such petty pain.

Prusias claimed that he had brought his master the cup of watered lemon juice as usual, picking up the tray from a serving area where it had been left for him and bringing it right to the study. The honorable Strabo had been alive when Prusias entered, and was still alive when he left. He had no idea how anyone could have sneaked in to stab his master and had seen no one loitering near the study. The other slaves backed him up on this:

those who had been around that day saw no one near the study, and none of them knew of any secret or subtle means to enter the building without being seen. Prusias said that he had never seen the knife before, and had no idea where it came from. The other slaves agreed.

After about an hour of this we left the slave pens and commenced a forced march across town to the Villa Strabo. It took the better part of an hour, but Quintilian didn't seem tired in the slightest when we arrived. When he's working on a problem, he notices neither hunger nor fatigue. We rounded the corner to the front of the villa and I saw a line of men stretching along the wall on both sides of the door. Among them were freedmen, citizens, and possibly even a few equestrians, judging by their garb. Some sat on the ground, some leaned against the wall, some just stood wringing their hands and looking sorrowful. Several clusters of them were engaged in what seemed to be heated conversation, with much arm waving and head shaking, nodding and thrusting forward. I sank gratefully to the ground while Quintilian knocked on the door. It was opened shortly by an older, full-stomached slave wearing imperial livery, and I pulled myself to my feet and stood in my accustomed place in Quintilian's shadow.

'Master Quintilian,' said the doorman, after looking my master over. 'Please come in.'

Quintilian peered at him. 'Thromax, isn't it? From the palace.'

Thromax nodded. 'The emperor sent a mob of us over to handle things until the — you know — gets straightened out.' He shook his head sadly. 'A horrible thing. When a slave kills his master it's bad for slaves everywhere.'

Quintilian patted him on the shoulder. 'You don't have to worry about that,' he said. 'Your master is, essentially, the state.'

'True, Master Quintilian,' Thromax said. 'I am lucky. My life is better than that of many people, and not all of them slaves.'

'Wisely said,' agreed Quintilian. 'The contented man is the one who can accept what the gods offer, knowing that wealth and poverty, happiness and misery, are just different spokes on the ever-turning wheel of life.'

'Easy to say if yours are the golden spokes,' Thromax commented.

'It is not too difficult to be a Stoic if you don't have much to be stoical about, that is so,' Quintilian agreed, smiling. He gestured toward the patient line of men outside the wall. 'Who are these men?'

'They are clients of the deceased Cassius Strabo,' Thromax said. 'There are at least thirty of them. It must be quite distressing for a client when his patron dies. Has he been left anything in the will? Will the son-and-heir take on his father's clients, or has he his own crowd of idlers and sycophants to take care of?' He stepped aside and waved us in; a regal gesture. 'I believe the undertakers are finished preparing the body, if you wish to say goodbye to your old friend.'

'I shall do that,' Quintilian said, letting Thromax take his wool cloak. He turned to me. 'Scribbler, go outside and rest. Do it near one of those groups of men and listen to what they are saying. They are certainly discussing the import of the events inside, and may well be a mirror of what the Roman public is thinking. Come to me by-and-by, when you have a sense of their emotions and desires.'

I touched my finger to my forehead in an oriental gesture of obedience, and went back outside. Tossing my sack of wax tablets on the ground, I resumed my slumping position against the wall of the villa, but this time closer to the nearest knot of gesticulating men. They continued their gesticulation, taking no notice of me.

I remained where I was, as my master had bidden, until I had a sense of the feelings of these men. It didn't take very long. 'Damn slaves should all be tied to posts and left to die,' said a thin, sharp-chinned man with evident satisfaction. 'Every last one of them. A long line of posts stretching east along the *Via Appia*, right outside the city.'

A fat man in a faded blue tunic raised his hands, palms outward, in mock horror. He had a red face and close-set eyes above puffy cheeks. 'You mean crucify them?' he asked shrilly. 'Punish some four hundred slaves, women and children too, for the act of one obviously demented servant?' He shook his head. 'What a waste! That's two or three thousand denarii worth of merchandise just slaughtered. And who's to pay for the crucifixions, I ask you?'

'Would you rather be murdered in your bed?' demanded the first man.

The two or three others in the group nodded their agreement, and one of them murmured, 'Quite right!'

I rose and wandered down the line to listen to some of the other conversations, and it was all like that. One man had the temerity to say, 'It doesn't seem fair somehow, that all those slaves should die, when they had nothing to do with the unfortunate murder.' He was shouted down. Another moaned, 'With the honorable Strabo dead, where am I to get the twenty denarii for my daughter's wedding? What a foul trick of the goddess Vesta to play on a humble man!' There was general sympathy for his plight, but I somehow felt that it was less than sincere.

I went inside and walked back to the peristylium, the large interior courtyard, to rejoin my master, who was just coming from viewing his old friend's body in what was usually the formal dining room, and related what I had heard.

'As I suspected,' he said. 'Sentiment is against us. And the people are becoming so inured to the sight of death by the gladiator games that the crucifying of four hundred slaves will merely seem one more spectacle for them to enjoy.'

There were people standing around in small groups in the courtyard talking quietly, as one does in the presence of the dead. Quintilian approached a small group of women sitting around a stone table and bowed to a strikingly handsome middle-aged lady. 'Madam Melissina,' he said.

'Master Quintilian.' She extended her hand. 'Last time we met was under happier circumstances.'

'I grieve along with you, Madam,' Quintilian told her. 'Your husband was a good friend, an upright and honorable man, and a true Roman.'

She bent her head slightly in agreement and thanks. 'My son has left to bring blankets and food to the slave pens. He told me you are going to see what you can do for us.'

'Of course I will,' Quintilian said. He studied her face intently. 'What is it,' he asked, 'that you think should be done?'

She thought about it for a minute. 'Can you show that Prusias did not do this thing?' she asked. 'For I cannot believe that he did. He has been with us since my husband was governor in Bithynia, and is one of our most trusted household slaves.' She put her hand on his arm. 'Barring that, can you somehow save the four hundred innocents?'

'I will do what I can, Madam. It is a mark of his quality of mind that your son Marius is able to consider such things at this time.'

'Yes, Marius,' she said. 'My poor son. This may kill him. If you do not succeed — it may kill him.'

'Madam?'

'Marius is — how to put this — enamored of a young slave girl.' Madam Melissina rose and, taking Quintilian by the elbow, led him to a bench where they both sat down. 'Do you understand?'

'I'm not sure. One of the household slaves is his mistress? He didn't mention this.'

'She is not his mistress,' Madam Melissina said. 'Edissa is, as far as I know, still a virgin.'

'Edissa?' Quintilian asked. 'Young, blonde, very comely?'

'That is she.'

'Ah!' Quintilian said. 'I saw her at the slave pens. I can well understand your son's infatuation.'

Madam Melissina rested her palms on her knees. 'Edissa is seventeen, very pretty, very sweet. She was sold into slavery by her parents when she was eleven. My sister Prunella bought her from a slave dealer after verifying that she was, ah, *intacta*. Slave dealers are not a trustworthy group. Edissa has been Prunella's personal maid for the past six years.'

'So she wasn't really the procurator's property?'

Madam Melissina sighed. 'Unfortunately,

my husband bought all of Prunella's property from her when she moved in with us a little over a year ago, after the death of her husband. A grove of fig trees that have ceased to bear figs, a house unfit to live in, and six slaves. It was a polite way of giving her some money, since she had none of her own. But I fear it was unlucky for Edissa.'

'And Marius?'

'Has been mooning over the girl since Prunella moved in.'

'But he hasn't done anything to, ah, formalize the relationship? Did his father disapprove?'

'Cassius knew nothing about it. My son suffers from a strange mixture of rectitude and desire. He wants the girl, but he wants her to come to him willingly.'

'It seems reasonable,' Quintilian said, 'that if given the choice between being your sister's body servant and being your son's well-loved concubine — '

'Yes,' Melissina agreed, 'but would it be love? Would the girl really love him, or just be taking the best of several unpalatable choices? If she were truly free to do as she chose, would she choose him? These are the questions that plague my son.'

Quintilian shook his head. 'How can one ever know the workings of another's mind?' he asked. 'Your son is chasing the impossible. And if he were to free her, and then woo her, might she not come to him out of gratitude or pity, rather than love?'

Melissina took his hand. 'We do not ask you to solve that problem, my dear Marcus,' she said. 'Only to spare her life — and that of the others.'

'We could devise something,' Quintilian said thoughtfully. 'The argument might be made that your sister never truly included Edissa in the sale. She has, I assume, remained Prunella's servant?'

'Yes,' Melissina said. 'But I'm afraid you'll have to devise something better than that.'

'I will?'

'Marius could not live with himself if he rescued Edissa but allowed all the others to be put to death.'

'It is not, after all, a question of allowing,' Quintilian said gently. 'If a ship is wrecked and fifty drown, but you manage to save one, do you berate yourself for not saving the others, or are you happy that you saved one?'

'If you're my son,' Melissina told him, 'you do your best to save them all — even if it means imposing on your friendship with the best lawyer in Rome — and hate yourself for caring more about one of them than all the rest.'

'Isn't he afraid that, should we succeed in saving this girl, she'll be grateful?'

'Probably,' Melissina said. 'But that's tomorrow's problem.'

'So it is,' Quintilian agreed. He pushed himself to his feet. 'I would like to speak to those who were out here when your husband's body was found,' he said. 'And examine the room he was in.'

'Of course,' Melissina said. 'I was in my workshop, but my sister and her daughter, Lucasta, were here in the courtyard the whole time.'

'Workshop?' Quintilian raised an eyebrow. I must practice doing that, it can convey a variety of emotions. This time it was polite enquiry.

'That's right, you didn't know,' Melissina

said. 'I've taken up sculpture in clay. The busts of my friends who are good enough to pose for me. I'm not very good, but I've only been doing it for a couple of months. At any rate, the workshop is quite around the other side of the villa, by the far wall. Not that there was anything I could have done had I been closer.' She reached her hand to her mouth, suppressing some emotion that a Roman matron shouldn't show. 'He was a good man, Marcus. Kind and generous to all around him. Honest and honorable. You know that.'

'I do,' Quintilian agreed.

'Come, speak to Prunella,' she said, and led him back to the group of women.

Prunella was a younger and slenderer version of her sister Melissina. 'My daughter Lucasta and I were here all that afternoon,' she told Quintilian. 'On that very bench,' she pointed, 'under that very tree. I'm teaching Lucasta Greek. Several of the slaves speak Greek, but their grammar is so bad I thought I'd better teach her myself. Whatever happened we must have seen, and yet we saw nothing unusual, nothing noteworthy — nothing.'

'Can you describe the events of that afternoon for me?' Quintilian asked, dropping into the seat beside her.

'As I said, nothing unusual happened — until dear Cassius's body was found.'

Quintilian nodded. 'Describe for me,' he said, 'the usual. Relate the events, however mundane, as they occurred.'

'Very well,' Prunella agreed. 'Where shall I start?'

'When did you arrive under that tree?'

Prunella closed her eyes and pressed her thumb to her chin thoughtfully. 'Shortly after lunch,' she said.

'Was the procurator in his study then?'

'No,' she said. 'He and the senator came out with us, as a matter of fact.'

'Senator Veccus?'

'That's the one.'

'I thought he found Cassius's body.'

'Oh, he did. That was much later. Cassius went into his study and Senator Veccus went off with his helmet.'

'His helmet?'

Prunella nodded. 'One of those centurion's helmets with the plume on it. The

162

two of them — Cassius and Senator Veccus — had been in a deep discussion over various aspects of it: the height of the crest, the width of the ear things — that sort of thing — all through lunch.' She waved her hands with a dismissive 'boys will be boys' air as she added, 'They seemed to think it was important.'

'Where did Veccus go?'

'As a matter of fact he came back to see me,' Madam Melissina said. 'In my workshop. He spent some time admiring my work. Rather more than it deserved, I thought. I think he wanted something from my husband and believed that my influence might be useful.'

'He came back after a while,' Prunella said, 'and sat over there, under that awning by the kitchen, and drank watered wine. He was fiddling with that helmet and occasionally pacing back and forth, as though trying to work something out in his head.'

'And all this time nobody came near the study?'

'Only Prusias. He picked up the tray from the table by the kitchen where the undercook had left it and took it in to his master. It was understood that nobody was to disturb Cassius while he was in his study.'

'You are sure you would have seen anyone?' Quintilian asked. 'You were not, perhaps, concentrating too strongly on your lessons? Greek can be very demanding.'

'I would have made use of the presence of anyone else,' Prunella said. 'I would have said, 'Look at that young boy slave going over to the study of your Uncle Cassius.' And she might have replied, 'He is tall for such a young man.' We were always looking for simple things to discuss in Greek, or perhaps I should say things to discuss with a simple vocabulary.'

'And you had no occasion to say any such thing?'

'None between the time Prusias brought the watered lemon juice and Senator Veccus found the procurator dead.'

'Which was about how long?'

'Perhaps two hours.'

'How did the senator find the body?'

'He said he had solved some problem with the — strap — flap? — on the helmet and he wanted to tell the procurator. He went to knock on the door, and got no answer. So he looked in at the window. I heard him cry, 'By the gods — Procurator Strabo has been stabbed!' and then push open the door. We all rushed after him, and there poor Cassius was, face down on the desk, dead of a knife thrust.' She bit her knuckle. 'It was horrible.'

'Thank you, madam,' Quintilian said. He rose. 'I would like to look at the study now.'

'If you must . . . ' said Melissina, rising to her feet with difficulty, as though a heavy weight were pressing her down. 'I will . . . '

'No need,' Quintilian said gently. 'Sit. Let your friends take some of the burden from you. I can manage.' He turned to me. 'Come,' he said.

Veni, vidi, I watched as Quintilian peered at the desk where poor Strabo had been killed, knocked at the plaster walls to make sure they were solid, and generally examined everything there was to be seen. 'Strabo must have been sitting here,' he said, sitting on the canvas camp chair before the desk. 'And he fell forward thus.' Quintilian collapsed suddenly onto the desk, his head among the papyri littering the desk.

'Yes, master,' I said. 'So it would seem.'

Quintilian sat up and looked around him. 'How odd,' he said.

'Yes, master,' I said.

'You see it then?'

I looked but saw not. 'No, master,' I said.

'The floor,' he said. 'The blood.'

There were dried patches of blood on the floor by the desk. I looked at them. They looked like dried patches of blood. 'The blood?' I asked.

'There is so little blood,' he said. 'And it's all on the floor by the desk here; none on the wall, or further along the floor. A very polite and orderly pool of blood, it would seem.'

'If you say so, Master Quintilian,' I said.

'I do.' He rose and looked around. 'Here,' he said, handing me a brass rule.

'What's this?'

'Your knife. You're to play Prusias. Now, you've just come in here with a tray' — he pulled a large copper plate from a shelf and handed it to me — 'and you have to put it on the edge of the desk and then stab me with the knife. Where are you going to keep the knife?'

I balanced the tray in one hand and held the knife in the other. 'Like this?'

'No. Remember, you have to cross the courtyard without anyone seeing the knife.'

'Oh.' I thought for a moment and then put the pseudo-knife flat under the tray. 'Here.'

'Possibly,' Quintilian allowed. 'But probably not. Remember, several of the people in the courtyard are sitting down. They might see the knife if you hold it under the tray.'

'That's so,' I agreed. After another moment's thought I put the plate down and fastened the brass rule under my tunic, holding it in place by tightening my belt.

'That will do,' Quintilian agreed. 'Now, come in with the tray, put it down, and attack me.' He sat back down in the chair and turned to the desk, picking up one of the papyri to read.

I picked up the plate and went to the door, then turned around and walked the three steps back to the desk, put down the tray and pulled the knife from inside my tunic. The side of the rule scraped my rib as I pulled it, and I was glad it wasn't the real knife.

Quintilian turned to me in mock horror and breathed, 'Prusias, old faithful retainer, what are you doing?'

'Org, org!' I said, and stabbed at him.

He rose from the chair and grabbed my arm, holding it easily in place even as I twisted to break free. 'This won't work,' he said, releasing my arm and sitting back down.

'Perhaps Prusias was stronger than I,' I suggested, 'or Procurator Strabo weaker than you.'

'Perhaps,' he said. 'But still . . . '

A great clamor arose from outside, and I went to the door. 'The emperor is here,' I said.

'Vespasian?' Quintilian stood up and

straightened his toga. A double squad of the Praetorian Guard had come into the courtyard and filed around the two sides. Then they turned and faced in, with much stamping of feet and slapping of arms, and stood at attention. Vespasian was already there, going up to the widow Strabo and taking her hand. Senator Veccus had arrived with the emperor, and was standing in the far doorway.

'Come,' Quintilian said. He walked out and crossed the courtyard. I followed behind.

'Fabius Quintilianus!' Vespasian called as we approached. 'Come to me, my old friend.'

'Greetings, General!' Quintilian said. Vespasian preferred the title of 'General' in private, and from those close to him. His old legionaries used it as a matter of course.

'I hear you've been examining some slaves at the pens, and in my name,' Vespasian said, looking stern.

'Indeed,' Quintilian replied. 'For is not the name of Vespasian synonymous with the name of justice?'

169

Vespasian laughed. 'Good response. How can I gainsay that? I told Senator Veccus when he complained about your interfering with the slaves that I knew nothing about it, but that anything Marcus Fabius Quintilianus did in my name was done with my approval whether I knew about it or not.'

'Thank you, Caesar,' said Quintilian, nodding deeply, but not quite bowing.

Vespasian reached out and held Quintilian's upper arm. 'There are few men that I can say that of,' he said. 'And I am pleased that you are one of them.' He released the arm. 'Now, what have you gotten me into? I can't really afford a fight with the Senate at this time.'

Senator Veccus had been approaching as they spoke, and Quintilian now turned to face him. 'No fight,' he told the emperor, 'and no mass execution of slaves either.'

'The Senate will insist,' said Vespasian.

'The Senate will insist on the murderer being punished,' Quintilian said. 'But the murderer was not a slave named Prusias, but a senator named Veccus.'

Senator Veccus stopped. 'What nonsense is this?' he cried, his voice perhaps a bit higher than he intended. 'You forget, I found the body. The procurator was already dead when I entered the room.'

'Indeed he was,' Quintilian agreed. 'Because you had poisoned him two hours before.'

'I? I had what?'

'You were sitting there' — my master pointed to the seat by the kitchen — 'and occasionally rising and pacing back and forth.' Quintilian waved his hand back and forth. 'Ample opportunity for you to drop some poison into the watered lemon juice before Prusias picked it up.'

'But,' objected Vespasian, 'the honorable Strabo was stabbed.'

'After his death, Caesar,' Quintilian said. 'There was far too little blood, and it was far too contained to have been shed while Strabo was alive. Veccus came to the window, cried out that Strabo had been stabbed, and then rushed in and did the job himself with a knife he had concealed under his toga. Since he had apparently found the honorable Strabo dead while he was still outside, no one would suspect him of having done it. And, since Strabo was stabbed, no one would suspect poison.'

'But why bother?' asked Vespasian.

'Yes,' Veccus inserted, 'why bother?'

'To divert attention from the fact that only two people could have poisoned the watered lemon juice,' Quintilian explained. 'Prusias the slave, or Veccus the senator. And, as everyone has said, Prusias had no reason.'

'And my reason?' Veccus demanded.

'I imagine it has something to do with that helmet you were playing with,' Quintilian said. 'Did the honorable Strabo find that you've been sending faulty helmets to the legions? We'll find out soon enough.'

'Bah!' Veccus said. 'I will listen to this nonsense no longer!' He wheeled about and stalked off toward the interior of the villa. No move was made to stop him. Where could he hide?

'Faulty equipment to the troops?' Vespasian grimaced. 'The man has dishonored the Senate and the people of Rome.'

I noted that the emperor had wholly accepted the truth of Quintilian's notices.

Such is the power of effective oratory.

'I will order the release of the slaves at once,' Vespasian said, 'and bring charges against Senator Veccus. Will you prosecute?'

'If you would have it so,' Quintilian replied.

There was a small commotion at the door to the house, and an imperial runner entered the courtyard and passed a rolled message to the centurion of the guard. He read it and then hastened over to Vespasian. 'General!' he said, holding the message out.

Vespasian took it and read it. Then he passed it over to my master. 'Too late,' he said.

Over Quintilian's shoulder I read: 'The slave Prusias from the household of the honorable Cassius Strabo has died of wounds inflicted under torture. The aedile Lepidus says it wasn't his fault.'

'Too late,' Quintilian agreed.

'The unnecessary death of an innocent man, even a slave, is a stain on the cloak of Roman justice,' the emperor Vespasian said.

'I couldn't have said it better,' said Quintilian.

'We will add that to the charge against Veccus.' Vespasian turned to his centurion. 'Take the senator into custody,' he said.

Madam Melissina, who was standing with us, dropped to her knees and pressed her forehead against the emperor's hand. 'Thank you, noble Caesar,' she said.

Vespasian looked embarrassed and pulled her to her feet. 'Please,' he said. 'You are the wife of my old and valued friend. Call me 'General.''

'Of course, General,' she replied. 'But I do thank you. And you, master Quintilian, for unraveling this knot and bringing the possibility of happiness into my son's life.'

Vespasian looked faintly puzzled. 'What's this?' he asked.

'I'll explain later,' Quintilian told him. 'For now . . . '

Two of the Praetorian Guard clattered into the courtyard. 'General,' the first called. 'Senator Veccus has taken his own life.'

'In the dining room,' said the other. 'With a knife.'

'There's blood all over the place,' added the first.

So the total was three dead. Was it the shrikes? Susannah maintains it was. Quintilian says that's superstitious nonsense. I reserve judgment. I'm not sure I believe, but as my old nurse used to say: '*Nuncus rebus mangus poppis; Halifratus satum flebis.*'

THE END

Other titles in the
Linford Mystery Library:

SNAKE EYES

Richard Hoyt

John Denson, the Seattle private eye
with his partner, Willie Prettybird — a
shaman of the Cowlitz tribe — face
their deadliest case: an engineered out-
break of anthrax in the Pacific Northwest.
A ballooning list of suspects includes a
rodeo cowboy; a barkeep with a roving
eye; an ancient teacher at a high-school
reunion — and the chief of police.
Then there's the fund-raising televan-
gelist Hamm Bonnerton. One of them
is playing liar's dice, and coming up
snake eyes. And killing people . . .

TERROR LOVE

Norman Lazenby

Married to Gilbert Brand, Kathryn imagines her marriage to be a happy one. It's studded with the parties of her husband's rich, socialite friends. But their attendance at a party given by his business associate, Victor Milo, tarnishes Brand's suave image. Kathryn discovers Brand attempting to strangle another guest, the nightclub singer Claudia, who becomes Kathryn's bitterest enemy. Then her world begins to crumble as she learns that Brand is an unscrupulous criminal . . . and she begins a descent into terror.